Merry Christmas Anne & Andrew

Love -

Uncle Debbie & Auntie Steve

The Old-Fashioned Storybook

Illustrated by Troy Allyn Howell

Selections by
Betty Ann Schwartz
and
Leon Archibald

Little Simon
Published by Simon & Schuster, Inc., New York

The
Old-Fashioned
Storybook

*To Donal, Chad, Cheree, Lavender, Troy, Johnny, Christopher,
and Olin—old-fashioned children in a modern time.*
—Troy Allyn Howell

Library of Congress Cataloging in Publication Data
Main entry under title:

The Old-fashioned storybook.

Summary: Twenty fairy tales from a variety of sources, including Grimm, Perrault, Andersen,
and Wilde.
1. Fairy tales.   2. Children's stories.
1. Fairy tales.   2. Folklore.   3. Short stories
I. Howell, Troy, ill.   II. Schwartz, Betty Ann.   III. Archibald, Leon.   IV. Title.
PZ8 04475 1985   398.2′1   85-6767
ISBN 0-671-55686-X
0-671-60721-9 (lib bdg.)
Illustrations Copyright ©
1985 Troy Allyn Howell
Published by LITTLE SIMON
A Simon & Schuster Division of Gulf & Western Corporation
Simon & Schuster Building, 1230 Avenue of the Americas, New York, New York 10020
Designed by Gill Speirs
Printed in the United States of America
10 9 8 7 6 5 4 3 2 1
LITTLE SIMON and colophon are trademarks of Simon & Schuster
Also available in Julian Messner Certified Edition

Contents

The
Old-Fashioned
Storybook

Little Red Cap

here was once a sweet little maid, much beloved by everybody, but most of all by her devoted grandmother, who could never do enough for her. Once the grandmother sent the girl a little cap of red velvet, and it was so very becoming to her that she never wore anything else. And so people began calling her Little Red Cap.

One day her mother said to her, "Come, Little Red Cap, here are some cakes and a flask of wine for you to take to Grandmother. She is weak and ill, and they will do her good. Make haste and start before it grows hot outside, but be sure to walk properly. Don't run, or you might fall and break the flask of wine. Then there would be none left for Grandmother. And when you go into her room, don't forget to say good morning, instead of staring about you."

"I will be sure to take care," said Little Red Cap to her mother.

Now the grandmother lived far away in the woods. When Little Red Cap reached the woods, she met a wolf. But she did not know what a dangerous sort of animal he was, so she did not feel frightened.

"Good day, Little Red Cap," said he.

"Good day, Wolf," answered she.

"Where are you going so early, Little Red Cap?"

"To my grandmother's."

"What are you carrying under your apron?"

"Cakes we baked yesterday, and some wine. My grand-mother is very weak and ill, so they will do her good and strengthen her."

"Where does your grandmother live, Little Red Cap?"

"Not far from here. Her house stands beneath the three oak trees, and you may know it by the hazel bushes," said Little Red Cap.

The wolf thought to himself, "That tender young thing would be a delicious morsel. I must manage somehow to eat her and her grandmother for my dinner."

Then he walked with Little Red Cap a while. "Little Red Cap, just look at the pretty flowers that are growing all round you. Stop and listen to the song of the birds. You are hurrying along just as if you were going to school, and it is so delightful out here in the woods, " he said to her.

Little Red Cap glanced round her. When she saw the sun-beams darting through the trees and the lovely flowers growing everywhere, she thought to herself, "If I were to take a fresh bou-quet to my grandmother, she would be very pleased. It is so early in the day that I shall still reach her in plenty of time if I stop." She picked one flower, then saw a prettier one a little farther off. She went quite far out of her way. But the wolf went straight to the grandmother's house and knocked at the door.

"Who is there?" cried the grandmother.

"Little Red Cap," the wolf answered, "and I have brought you some cake and wine. Please open the door."

"Lift the latch," cried the grandmother. "I am too feeble to get up from the bed."

So the wolf lifted the latch. The door flew open and he fell on the grandmother and ate her up without saying one word. Then he put on her clothes and her cap, lay down in her bed, and drew the curtains.

All this time Little Red Cap was running among the flowers. When she had gathered as many as she could hold, she remembered her grandmother and set off to go to her. She was surprised to find the door standing open. When she went inside she felt very strange, and thought to herself, "Oh dear, how uncomfortable I feel, and just this morning I was so glad to go to my grandmother!"

When Little Red Cap said good morning, there was no answer. Then she went up to the bed and drew back the curtains. There lay the grandmother with her cap pulled down to her eyes, so that she looked very odd.

"O Grandmother, what large ears you have!"

"The better to hear you with."

"O Grandmother, what great eyes you have!"

"The better to see you with."

"O Grandmother, what large hands you have!"

"The better to take hold of you with."

"But Grandmother, what a terrible, large mouth you have!"

"The better to eat you with!" And no sooner had the wolf said that than he made one bound from the bed and swallowed up poor Little Red Cap.

Then the wolf, having satisfied his hunger, lay down again in the bed, went to sleep, and began to snore loudly. The huntsman heard him as he was passing by the house, and he thought, "How the old woman snores! I had better see if there is anything the matter with her."

Then he went into the room, walked up to the bed, and saw the wolf lying there.

"At last I find you, you old sinner!" said the huntsman. "I have been looking for you a long time."

And he made up his mind that the wolf had swallowed the grandmother whole, and that she might yet be saved. So he did not fire his gun. Instead he took a pair of shears and began to slit the wolf's body. When he made a few snips, Little Red Cap appeared. After a few more snips, she jumped out and cried, "Oh dear, how frightened I have been! It is so dark inside the wolf." And then out came the old grandmother, still living and breathing. But Little Red Cap went and quickly fetched some large stones, with which she filled the wolf's body. So when he woke up

and tried to rush away, the stones were so heavy that he sank down and fell dead.

They were all three very pleased. The huntsman took off the wolf's skin and carried it home. The grandmother ate the cakes, drank the wine, and felt better again. And Little Red Cap said to herself that she would nevermore stray about in the woods alone, talking to strangers.

Tom Thumb

here was once a poor countryman who used to sit in the chimney corner all evening and poke the fire, while his wife sat at her spinning-wheel. And he used to say, "How dull it is without any children about us. Our house is so quiet, and other people's houses are so noisy and merry!"

"Yes," answered his wife, and sighed. "If we could only have a child, even a little one, no bigger than my thumb, how happy I would be!"

It happened that after a while the woman did have a child who was perfect in all his limbs, but who was no bigger than a thumb. Then the parents said, "He is just what we wished for, and we will love him very much." And they gave him a name to match his size: Tom Thumb. Though they gave him plenty of nourishment, he remained exactly the same size as when he was first born. But Tom Thumb had very good faculties. He was very quick and prudent, so that everything he did turned out right.

One day his father prepared to go into the forest to cut wood, and he said, as if to himself, "I wish there were someone to bring the cart to meet me."

"Oh, Father," cried Tom Thumb. "I can bring the cart all by myself, and in proper time, too!"

The father laughed at this and said, "How will you manage that? You are much too little to hold the reins."

"That has nothing to do with it, Father. I will sit in the horse's ear and tell him where to go."

"Well," answered the father, "we will try it once."

The mother set Tom Thumb in the horse's ear, and so he drove off, crying, "Gee-up, gee-wo!"

The horse went on quite as if his master were driving him. He drew the wagon along the road to the wood.

Now it happened that just as they were turning a corner, and Tom Thumb was calling out "Gee-up" in the horse's ear, two strange men passed by. "Look," said one of them. "How is this? There goes a wagon, and the driver is calling to the horse, yet he is nowhere to be seen!"

"It is very strange," said the other. "We will follow the wagon and see where it goes."

The wagon went right through the wood, up to the place where the wood had been cut. When Tom Thumb caught sight of his father, he cried out, "Look, Father, here am I with the wagon! Now take me down."

The father took his little son out of the horse's ear, and Tom Thumb sat down on a stump, quite happy and content. When the two strangers saw him they were struck dumb with wonder. At last, one of them took the other aside and said to him, "Look here, the little chap would make us a fortune if we were to show him in the town for money. Suppose we buy him."

So they went up to the woodcutter and said, "Sell the little man to us. We will take care he shall come to no harm."

"No," answered the father. "He is the apple of my eye, and not for all the money in the world would I sell him."

But when Tom Thumb heard what was going on, he jumped onto his father's coattails, climbed all the way up to his shoulder, and whispered in his ear, "Father, you might as well let me go. I will soon come back again."

So the father gave his little son up to the two men for a great deal of money.

The men asked Tom Thumb where he would like to sit. "Oh,

put me on the brim of your hat," said he. "There I can walk about and view the country."

So they did as he wished, and when Tom Thumb had taken leave of his father, the three set off together. They traveled on until dusk, and the little fellow asked to be set down awhile. At first his companions said no, but soon they agreed. So the man took Tom Thumb down from his hat and set him in a field by the roadside.

Quickly Tom Thumb ran away into the furrows, and slipped suddenly into a mouse hole—just what he was looking for.

"Good evening, my masters. You can go home without me!" he told them, laughing. They took turns feeling about with their sticks in the mouse hole, but it was in vain. Tom Thumb crept farther and farther in. As it was growing dark, they had to make the rest of their way home, full of anger and with empty purses.

When Tom Thumb found they were gone, he crept out of his underground hiding place. He heard two men pass by, and one was saying to the other, "How can we manage to get hold of the rich parson's gold and silver?"

"I can tell you how," cried Tom Thumb.

"What is this?" said one of the thieves, quite frightened. "I hear someone speak!"

So they stood still and listened, and Tom Thumb spoke again.

"Take me with you. I will show you how to do it!"

"Where are you, then?" asked they.

"Look about on the ground and notice where the voice comes from," answered he.

At last they found him and lifted him up.

"You little elf," said they. "How can you help us?"

"Look here," answered he. "I can easily creep between the iron bars of the parson's room and hand out to you whatever you would like to have."

"Very well," said they. "We will see what you can do."

So they came to the parsonage house. But when Tom Thumb crept into the room, he cried out with all his might, "Will you have all that is here?"

The thieves were terrified and said, "Do speak more softly,

lest anyone should be awakened."

But Tom Thumb made as if he did not hear them. He cried out again, "What would you like? Will you have all that is here?" At that, the cook, who was sleeping in a room nearby, heard the loud voice and raised herself in bed to listen.

Thinking Tom Thumb might be joking, the thieves whispered to him to be serious and to hand them out something. But Tom Thumb called out once more as loud as he could, "Oh yes, I will give it all to you if you put out your hands."

Then the listening maid jumped out of bed and burst open the door. The thieves ran off as if a wild huntsman were behind them. But the maid could see nothing in the dark, so she went to fetch a light. And when she came back with one, Tom Thumb had taken off into the barn, without being seen by her. The maid, when she had looked in every corner and found nothing, went back to bed at last, thinking that she must have been dreaming.

So Tom Thumb crept among the hay and found a comfortable nook to sleep in. He thought he would remain there until it was day and then go home to his father and mother. But other things were to befall him—indeed, there is nothing but trouble and worry in this world! The maid got up at dawn to feed the cows. The first place she went to was the barn, where she took up an armful of hay, and it happened to be the very heap in which Tom Thumb lay asleep. He was so fast asleep that he was aware of nothing. He never awoke until he was in the mouth of the cow, who had eaten him up with the hay.

"Oh dear," cried Tom Thumb, "What is all this tossing and tumbling? Have I gotten into a mill?" But he soon figured out where he was. He had to be very careful not to get between the cow's teeth. Since he couldn't get out the way he'd come, he had to descend into the cow's stomach.

"The windows were forgotten when this little room was built," said he, in the dark stomach.

His quarters were in every way unpleasant to him, and worst of all, new hay was constantly coming in to fill up the space even more. At last he cried out as loud as he could, "No more hay for me! No more hay for me!"

The maid was milking the cow when she heard the voice. But as she could see no one, and as it was the same voice that she had heard in the night, she was so frightened that she fell off her stool and spilt the milk. Then she ran in great haste to her master, crying, "Oh, master dear, the cow spoke!"

"You must be crazy," answered the parson, and he went himself to the cow barn to see what was the matter. No sooner had he put his foot inside the door than Tom Thumb cried out again, "No more hay for me! No more hay for me!"

Then the parson himself was frightened, thinking that a bad spirit had entered into the cow, and he ordered the cow to be put to death. So she was killed, but the stomach, with Tom Thumb inside, was thrown upon a dunghill.

Tom Thumb had great trouble working his way out of the stomach. He had just made a space big enough for his head to go through when a new misfortune happened. A hungry wolf ran up and swallowed the whole stomach at one gulp. But Tom Thumb did not lose courage. "Perhaps the wolf will listen to reason," thought he, and he cried out from inside the wolf, "My dear wolf, I can tell you where to get a splendid meal!"

"Where is it to be had?" asked the wolf.

"In a house I know. You must creep into it through a drain, and there you will find cakes and bacon and broth, as much as you can eat," and he described his father's house.

The wolf didn't need to be told twice. He went to the house at night, squeezed himself through the drain, and feasted in the storeroom to his heart's content. When at last he was satisfied, he wanted to go away again. But he had become so big that to creep the same way back was impossible. Tom Thumb had reckoned upon this, and he began to make a terrible din inside the wolf, crying and calling as loud as he could.

"Be quiet!" said the wolf. "You will wake the folks up!"

"Look here," cried the little man. "You are very well satisfied, and now I will do something for my own enjoyment." And he began again to make all the noise he could. At last the father and mother were awakened, and they hurried to the storeroom door and peeped through the chink. When they saw a wolf there, they ran and fetched weapons—the man an ax and the wife a scythe.

"Stay behind," said the man as they entered the room. "If a blow from my ax does not kill him, then you must cut at him with your scythe."

Tom Thumb heard his father's voice, and cried, "Father dear, I am here in the wolf's insides."

Then the father called out, full of joy, "Thank heaven that we have found our dear child!" He drew near and struck the wolf such a blow on the head that the wolf fell down dead. Then he fetched a knife and a pair of scissors, slit up the wolf's body, and let out the little fellow.

"Oh, how worried we have been about you!" said the father.

"Yes, Father, I have seen a good deal of the world, and I am very glad to breathe fresh air again."

"And where have you been all this time?" asked his father.

"Oh, I have been in a mouse hole, a cow's stomach, and a wolf's insides. Now, I think, I will stay at home."

"And we will not part with you for all the kingdoms of the world," cried his parents as they kissed and hugged their dear little Tom Thumb.

The Ugly Duckling

T he country was very lovely that summer. The wheat was golden and the oats still green. The hay was stacked in the rich low meadows, where the stork marched about on his long red legs, chattering in Egyptian, the language his mother had taught him.

Round about the field and meadow grew great woods, in the midst of which were deep lakes. In the sunniest spot stood an old mansion surrounded by a deep moat. Great leaves grew from the walls of the house right down to the water's edge. Some of the leaves were so tall that a small child could stand upright under them. In among them it was as secluded as in the depths of a forest. There a duck was sitting on her nest. Her little ducklings were just about to be hatched, but she was quite tired of sitting, for she had been there such a long time. Moreover, she had had very few visitors, as the other ducks liked swimming about in the moat better than waddling up to sit under the leaves and gossip with her.

At last one egg after another began to crack. "Cheep, cheep!" came the sound from the cracks. All the chicks had come to life and were poking their heads out.

"How big the world is, to be sure!" said all the young ones. They certainly had ever so much more room to move about now than when they were inside their eggshells.

"Do you imagine this is the whole world?" said the mother. "It stretches a long way on the other side of the garden right into the parson's field, though I have never been as far as that. I suppose you are all here now?" She got up and looked about. "No, I declare I have not hatched you all yet! The biggest egg is still there. How long is this going to take?" she said, and settled herself on the nest again.

"Well, how are you getting on?" said an old duck who had come to pay her a visit.

"This one egg is taking such a long time!" answered the sitting duck. "The shell will not crack. But you must look at the others. They are the finest ducklings I have ever seen. They are all exactly like their father, yet he never comes to see me, the rascal!"

"Let me look at the egg that won't crack," said the old duck. "You may be sure that it is a turkey's egg! I was cheated like that once. I had no end of trouble and worry with the creature, for I may tell you that he was afraid of water. I simply could not get him into it. I quacked and snapped at him, but it all did no good. Let me see the egg! Yes, it is a turkey's egg. You just leave it alone, and teach the other children to swim."

"I will sit on it a little longer," said the mother.

"Please yourself," said the old duck, and away she went.

At last the big egg cracked. "Cheep, cheep!" said the young one and tumbled out. How big and ugly he was! The duck looked at him.

"That is a monstrously big duckling," she said. "None of the others looked like that. Can he be a turkey chick? Well, we shall soon find that out. Into the water he shall go, if I have to kick him in myself."

Splash! into the water she sprang. "Quack, quack," she said, and one duckling plunged in after the other. The water dashed over their heads, but they came up again and floated beautifully. Their legs started to paddle, and they all learned to swim together. Even the big, ugly gray one swam about with them.

"No, that is no turkey," the mother said. "See how beautifully he uses his legs and how erect he holds himself. He is my own chick, after all, and not bad-looking when you come to look at him properly. Quack, quack! Now come with me and I will take you out into the world. But keep close to me all the time so that no one will tread upon you. Now into the moat, and use your legs," said she. "And mind you, quack properly."

They did as they were bid, but the other ducks round about looked at them and said, quite loudly, "Just look there! Now we are to have that tribe join us, as if there were not enough of us already. And, oh dear, how ugly that duckling is! We won't stand him." A duck flew at the duckling and bit him in the neck.

"Let him be," said the mother. "He is doing no harm."

"Very likely not," said the biter. "But he is so ungainly and queer that he must be whacked."

Just then they swam by the grandest, oldest duck in the moat.

"Those are handsome children the mother has," said she. "They are all good-looking except this one, who is not a fine specimen. It's a pity you can't make him over again."

"That can't be done, Your Grace," said the mother duck. "He is not handsome, but he is a thoroughly good creature, and he swims as beautifully as any of the others. I think I might venture even to add that I think he will improve with age." And then she patted his neck and stroked him. "Besides, he is a drake," said she. "So it does not matter so much. I believe he will be very strong, and I don't doubt but he will make his way in the world."

So the first day passed, and afterward matters grew worse and worse. The poor duckling was chased and badgered by all of the others. Even his brothers and sisters ill-used him. They were always saying, "If only the cat would get hold of you, you hideous object!" His own mother said, "I wish to goodness you were miles away." The ducks bit him, the hens pecked him, and the girls who fed the ducks kicked him aside. When he ran off and flew right over the hedge where the little birds were nesting, they flew up into the air in a fright.

"That is because I am so ugly," thought the poor duckling, shutting his eyes. He ran until he came to a great marsh where the wild ducks lived. He was so tired and miserable that he stayed there the whole night. In the morning the wild ducks flew up to inspect their new comrade.

"What sort of creature are you?" they inquired, as the duckling turned from side to side and greeted them as well as he could. "You are frightfully ugly," said the wild ducks, "but that does not matter to us, so long as you do not marry into our family." Poor fellow! He had not thought of marriage. All he wanted was permission to lie among the rushes and to drink a little of the marsh water.

He stayed there two whole days. Then two wild geese came, who were not long out of the shell and therefore rather pert.

"I say, comrade," they honked, "you are so ugly that we have taken quite a fancy to you! Will you join us and be a bird of passage? There is another marsh close by, and there are some charming wild geese there. All are sweet young ladies who can say quack!" Just at that moment, *bang! bang!* was heard among the reeds, and the water turned blood red. *Bang! bang!* went the guns, and flocks of wild geese flew from the rushes as the shots peppered among them.

The retrieving dogs wandered about in the swamp—*splash! splash!* The rushes and reeds bent on all sides beneath the dogs' treads. It was terribly alarming to the poor duckling. He twisted his head around to get it under his wing. Just at that moment a frightful dog appeared close beside him. His tongue hung right out of his mouth and his eyes glared wickedly. He opened his great mouth right next to the duckling, showed his sharp teeth, and—*splash!*—went on without touching him.

"Oh, thank heaven!" sighed the duckling. "I am so ugly that even the dog won't bite me!"

Then he lay quite still while the shots whistled among the bushes, and *bang* after *bang* rent the air. It only became quiet late in the day, but even then the poor duckling did not dare to get up. He waited several hours more before he looked about, and then he hurried away from the marsh as fast as he could, running across fields and meadows. Soon the wind began to whistle so fiercely around the duckling that he had to sit on his tail to resist it, and it blew harder and even harder.

Toward night he reached a poor little cottage. It was such a miserable hovel that it could not even make up its mind which way to fall, and so it remained standing. The duckling saw that the door had fallen off one hinge and hung so crookedly that he could creep into the house through the crack. That was how he made his way into the room.

An old woman lived there with her cat and her hen. The cat, whom she called Sonnie, would arch his back, purr, and give off electric sparks if you stroked his fur the wrong way. The hen had quite tiny, short legs, and so she was called Chickie-Low-Legs. She laid good eggs, and the old woman was as fond of her as she would have been of her own child.

"What on earth is that?" said the old woman, looking around. But her sight was not good and she thought the duckling was a fat duck. "This is a wonderful find!" said she. "Now I shall have duck's eggs. If only it is not a drake. We must wait and see about that."

So she let the duckling stay for three weeks, but no eggs made their appearance.

Now the cat was master of this house and the hen its mistress. They always thought that they represented the half of the world, and quite the better half.

The duckling thought there might be two opinions on the subject, but the cat would not hear of it.

"Can you lay eggs?" asked the hen.

"No."

"Have the goodness to hold your tongue then!" And then the cat asked, "Can you arch your back, purr, or give off sparks?"

"No."

"Then you had better keep your opinions to yourself when people of sense are speaking!"

The duckling sat in the corner nursing his hurt. Then he began to think of the fresh air and the sunshine, and an uncontrollable longing to float on the water seized him. At last he could not help telling the hen about it.

"What on earth possesses you?" she asked. "You have nothing to do. That is why you get these strange ideas into your head. Lay some eggs or take to purring, and you will get over it."

"But it is so delicious to float on the water," said the duckling. "It is so delicious to feel it rushing over your head when you dive to the bottom."

"That would be a fine amusement!" said the hen. "I think you have gone mad. Ask the cat about it. He is the wisest creature I know. Ask him if he is fond of floating on the water or diving under it. I say nothing about myself. Ask our mistress herself, the old woman. There is no one in the world cleverer than she is. Do you suppose she has any desire to float on the water or to duck underneath it?"

"You do not understand me," said the duckling. "I think I will go out into the wide world."

"Oh, do so by all means," said the hen.

So away went the duckling. He floated on the water and ducked underneath it, but he continued to be laughed at by every living creature for his ugliness.

Soon autumn came. The leaves in the woods turned yellow and brown. The wind took hold of them and they danced about. The sky looked very cold and the clouds hung heavy with snow and hail.

One evening the sun was just setting in wintry splendor when a flock of beautiful, large birds appeared out of the bushes. The duckling had never seen anything so wonderful. They were dazzling white swans, with long, waving necks. Uttering a peculiar cry, they spread out their magnificent, broad wings and flew away from the cold regions to warmer lands and open seas. They mounted so high, so very high, that the ugly little duckling became strangely uneasy. He circled round and round in the water like a wheel, craning his neck up into the air after them. Then he uttered a shriek so piercing and so strange that he was quite frightened by it himself. Oh, he could not forget those beautiful birds, those happy birds. And as soon as they were out of sight, he ducked right down to the bottom of the pond, and when he came up again he was quite beside himself. He did not know what the birds were or whither they flew, but all the same he was more drawn toward them than he had ever been by any creatures he had seen before.

The winter was so bitterly cold that the duckling had to swim about to keep the water around him from freezing over. But every night the hole in which he swam got smaller and smaller. At last he was so weary that he could move no more, and he was frozen fast into the ice.

Early in the morning a peasant came along and saw him. He went out onto the ice, cut a hole in it, and carried the duckling home to his wife. There the duckling soon revived. The children wanted to play with him, but the duckling thought they were going to mistreat him, so he rushed in fright into the milk pan, and the milk spurted out all over the room. The woman shrieked and threw up her hands. Then he flew into the butter cask, escaping only to fall down into the meal tub. Just imagine what he looked like by this time! The woman screamed and tried to hit him with the tongs. The children tumbled over one another in trying to catch him, and they screamed with laughter. By good luck the door stood open, and the duckling flew out among the bushes and the newly fallen snow. And he lay there thoroughly exhausted.

But it would be too sad to mention all the misery he had to go through during the hard winter. When the sun began to shine warmly again, the duckling was in the marsh, lying among the rushes. The larks were singing and the beautiful spring had come.

Then all at once the duckling raised his wings, and they flapped with much greater strength than before. They bore him vigorously. Before he knew where he was, he found himself in a large garden where the apple trees were in full blossom and the air was scented with lilacs, the long branches of which overhung the shores of the lake. Oh, the spring freshness was delicious!

Just in front of him he saw three beautiful white swans. They advanced toward him from a thicket. With rustling feathers they swam lightly over the water. The duckling recognized the majestic birds, and he was overcome by a strange melancholy.

HE SAW
BELOW HIM
HIS OWN
IMAGE

"I will fly to those royal birds and they will hack me to pieces because I, who am so ugly, venture to approach them. But it won't matter! Better to be killed by them than be snapped at by the ducks, pecked by the hens, spurned by the henwife, or suffer so much misery in the winter."

So he flew into the water and swam toward the stately swans. They saw him and darted toward him with ruffled feathers.

"Kill me!" said the poor creature, and he bowed his head toward the water and awaited his death. But what did he see reflected in the transparent water?

He saw below him his own image, but he was no longer a clumsy, dark gray bird, ugly and ungainly. He was himself a swan! After all, it does not matter in the least having been born in a duckyard, if only you come out of a swan's egg!

The big swans swam around him, stroking him with their bills. Some little children came into the garden with corn and pieces of bread to throw into the water, and the smallest one cried out, "There is a new one!" The other children shouted with joy, "Yes, a new one has come." And they clapped their hands and danced about, running after their father and mother. They threw the bread into the water, and one and all said, "The new one is the prettiest of them all. He is so young and handsome."

The duckling—who was now a swan—felt quite shy, and hid his head under his wing. He did not know what to think. He was very happy, but not at all proud, for a good heart never becomes proud. He thought of how he had been chased and scorned, and now he heard them all say that he was the most beautiful of all beautiful birds. The lilacs bent their boughs right down into the water before him, and the bright sun was warm and cheering. He rustled his feathers and raised his slender neck aloft, saying with exultation in his heart, "I never dreamt of so much happiness when I was the ugly duckling!"

The Witch

Once upon a time there was a peasant whose wife died, leaving him with two children. They were twins—a boy and a girl. For some years the poor man lived alone with the children, caring for them as best he could. But without a wife to help look after the house, everything in it seemed to go wrong. At last he made up his mind to marry again, feeling that a wife would bring peace and order to his household and take care of his motherless children.

So he married, and in the following years several more children were born to him. But peace and order did not come to the household, for the stepmother was very cruel to the twins. She beat them and half-starved them and constantly drove them out of the house, for her one idea was to get them out of the way. All day she thought of nothing but how she should get rid of them. At last an evil idea came into her head: she determined to send them out into the great, gloomy woods where a wicked witch lived. And so one morning she spoke to them, saying, "You have been such good children that I am going to send you to visit my granny, who lives in a dear little hut in the woods. You will have to wait upon her and serve her, but you will be well rewarded, for she will give you the best of everything."

So the children left the house together; and the little sister, who was very wise for her years, said to the brother, "We will first go and see our own dear grandmother, and tell her where our stepmother is sending us."

And when the grandmother heard where they were going, she cried and said, "You poor motherless children! How I pity you, and yet I can do nothing to help you! Your stepmother is not sending you to her granny, but to a wicked witch who lives in that great, gloomy woods. Now listen to me, children. You must be polite and kind to everyone, and never say a cross word to anyone, and never touch a crumb belonging to anyone else. Who knows if, after all, help may not be sent to you?"

She gave her grandchildren a bottle of milk, a piece of ham, and a loaf of bread, and they set out for the great, gloomy woods. In the thickest of the trees, they saw a queer little hut. And when they looked into it, there sat the witch.

"Who's there?" she snarled in an awful voice when she saw the children.

And they answered politely, though they were so terrified that each tried to hide behind the other.

"Good morning, Granny. Our stepmother has sent us to wait upon you and serve you."

"See that you do it well, then," growled the witch. "If I am pleased with you, I'll reward you; but if I am not, I'll put you in a pan and fry you in the oven—that's what I'll do with you, my pretty dears! You have been gently reared, but you'll find my work hard enough. See if you don't."

And so saying, she set the girl spinning yarn and gave the boy a sieve in which to carry water from the well. She herself went out into the woods. The girl wept bitterly because she did not know how to spin. Suddenly, she heard the sound of hundreds of little feet, and from every hole and corner in the hut, mice came pattering along the floor, squeaking and saying:

> "Little girl, why are your eyes so red?
> If you want help, then give us some bread."

And the girl gave them the bread that her grandmother had

THEY HEARD THE SOUND OF THE BROOM

given her. Then the mice told her that the witch had a cat, and the cat was very fond of ham; if she would give the cat her ham, the cat would show her the way out of the wood. In the meantime they would spin the yarn for her.

So the girl set out to look for the cat, and as she was hunting about, she met her brother. He was in great trouble because he could not carry water from the well in a sieve, as it came pouring out as fast as he put it in. She was trying to comfort him when they heard a rustling of wings. On the ground beside them alighted a flight of wrens who said:

"Give us some crumbs, then you need not grieve.
For you'll find that water will stay in the sieve."

So the twins crumbled their bread on the ground, and the wrens pecked it, and chirruped and chirped. When they had eaten the last crumb, they told the boy to fill up the holes of the sieve with clay, and then to draw water from the well. So he did what they said and carried the sieve full of water into the hut without spilling a drop. When the twins entered the hut, they found the cat curled up on the floor. So they stroked her, fed her ham, and said to her, "Pussy, gray pussy, tell us how we are to get away from the witch."

The cat thanked them for the ham, gave them a pocket handkerchief and a comb, and told them that when the witch pursued them, as she certainly would, all they had to do was to throw the handkerchief on the ground and run as fast as they could. As soon as the handkerchief touched the ground, a deep, broad river would spring up, right in the witch's path. If she managed to get across it, they must throw the comb behind them and run for their lives, for where the comb fell a dense forest would start up, which would delay the witch so long that they would be able to get safely away.

The cat had scarcely finished speaking when the witch returned to see if the children had fulfilled their tasks.

"Well, you have done well enough for today," she grumbled, "but tomorrow you'll have something more difficult to do, and if you don't do it well, you pampered brats, straight into the oven you go."

Half-dead with fright and trembling in every limb, the poor children lay down to sleep on two heaps of straw in the corner of the hut; but they dared not close their eyes and scarcely ventured to breathe. In the morning the witch gave the girl two pieces of linen to weave before night. To the boy she gave a pile of wood to cut into chips. Then the witch left them to their tasks and went out into the woods. As soon as she had gone out of sight, the children took the comb and the handkerchief, and they started to run. They met a watchdog who was going to leap on them and tear them to pieces, but they threw the remains of their bread to him, and he ate that and wagged his tail. Then they ran into the birch trees. The branches scratched the children's faces. But the little sister tied the twigs together with a piece of ribbon, and so they got past safely. At last, after running through the woods, they came out onto the open fields.

In the meantime at the hut the cat was busy weaving the linen. Soon the witch returned to see how the children were getting on, and she crept up to the window and whispered, "Are you weaving, my little dear?"

"Yes, Granny, I am weaving," answered the cat.

When the witch saw that the children had escaped her, she was furious, and she hit the cat with a metal pot, saying, "Why did you let the children leave the hut? Why did you not scratch their eyes out?"

But the cat curled up its tail, put its back up, and answered, "I have served you all these years and you have never even thrown me a bone, but the dear children gave me their own piece of ham."

Then the witch was furious with the watchdog and with the birch trees because they had let the children pass. But the dog answered, "I have served you all these years and you have never given me so much as a hard crust, but the dear children gave me their own loaf of bread."

And the birches rustled their leaves and said, "We have served you longer than we can say, and you have never even tied a bit of twine round our branches; but the dear children bound them up with their brightest ribbons."

So the witch saw that there was no help to be gotten from her old servants, and that the best thing she could do was to mount her old broom and set off in pursuit of the children. As the children ran they heard the sound of the broom sweeping the ground close behind them. Instantly the boy threw the handkerchief down over his shoulder. In a moment a deep, broad river flowed behind them.

When the witch came up to it, it took her a long time before she found a place which she could cross over on her broomstick. Her broom was tired from pursuing the children and could no longer go very high. But at last she got across and continued the chase faster than before.

As the children ran they heard a sound. The little sister put her ear to the ground and heard the broom sweeping the earth close behind them. So, quick as a thought, she threw the comb down on the ground. In an instant, as the cat had said, a dense forest sprang up, in which the roots and branches were so closely intertwined that it was impossible to force a way through it. So when the witch came up to it on her broom she found that there was nothing she could do but turn round and go back to her hut.

The twins ran straight on till they reached their own home. When they told their father all that they had suffered, he became so angry with their stepmother that he drove her out of the house and never let her return. From then on, he and the children lived happily together; and he took care of them himself and never let a stranger come near them.

The Princess and the Pea

here was once upon a time a prince who wanted to marry a princess, but only if she were a true princess. So he traveled through the whole world to find one, and even though there seemed to be plenty of princesses, he could not find one *true* princess. In every case, there was some little defect that showed the genuine article had not yet been found. So he came home in very low spirits, for he had wanted very much to marry a true princess.

One night there was a dreadful storm; there was thunder and lightning, and the rain streamed down in torrents. A knocking was suddenly heard at the palace gate, and the old queen went to open it.

There stood a princess outside the gate; but oh, in what a sad plight she was from the rain and the storm! The water was running down from her hair and her dress into the points of her shoes and out at the heels again. And yet, bedraggled though she was, she said she was a true princess!

"Well, we shall soon find out about that!" thought the old queen. But she said nothing. Instead, the queen went into the room where the girl was to sleep. She took off all the bedclothes and laid a pea on the bottom of the bed. Then she put twenty mattresses on top of the pea, and twenty eiderdown quilts on the

SHE
WAS A
TRUE
PRINCESS

TROY · ALLYN · HOWELL

top of the mattresses. And this was the bed in which the princess was to sleep.

The next morning the old queen asked how the girl had slept.

"Oh, very badly!" said the princess. "I scarcely closed my eyes all night! I am sure I don't know what was in the bed. I lay on something so hard that my whole body is black and blue. It is dreadful!"

And so they knew that she was a true princess, because she had felt the pea through the twenty mattresses and twenty eiderdown quilts. No one but a true princess could be so sensitive.

So the prince married her because at last he had met the true princess for whom he had been looking. And the pea was put into the Royal Museum, where it is still to be seen if no one has stolen it. Now this is a true story.

Thumbelina

here was once a woman who wanted to have a tiny child, but she did not know where to get one. So one day she went to an old witch and said to her, "I should so much like to have a tiny child; can you tell me where I can get one?"

"Oh, we have one ready!" said the witch. "Here is a barleycorn for you. Put it in a flowerpot and then you will see something happen."

"Oh, thank you!" said the woman, and she gave the witch a shilling, for that was what it cost. Then she went home and planted the barleycorn. Immediately there grew out of it a large and beautiful flower that looked like a tulip, but the petals were tightly closed as if it were still only a bud.

"What a beautiful flower!" exclaimed the woman, and she kissed the red and yellow petals. But as she kissed them the flower burst open. It was a real tulip, such as one can see any day; but in the middle of the blossom, on the green, velvety petals, sat a little girl, quite tiny, trim, and pretty. She was scarcely half a thumb in height, so they called her Thumbelina. An elegant, polished walnut shell served Thumbelina as a cradle, the blue petals of a violet were her mattress, and a rose petal was her coverlet. At night she would lie in this cradle, but in the daytime she liked to play about on the table. There the woman had put a bowl, surrounded by a ring of flowers, in the middle of which floated a great tulip petal. On this petal Thumbelina sat and sailed from one side of the bowl to the other, rowing herself with two white horsehairs for oars. It was such a pretty sight! She could sing, too, with a voice more soft and sweet than had ever been heard before in the land.

One night, when she was lying in her pretty little bed, an old toad crept in through a broken pane in the window. She was very ugly, clumsy, and clammy, and she hopped onto the table where Thumbelina lay asleep under the red rose petal.

"She would make a beautiful wife for my son," said the toad, taking up the walnut shell with Thumbelina inside and hopping with it through the window into the garden.

A great, wide stream, with slippery and marshy banks, flowed there. This was where the toad lived with her son. Ugh! How ugly and clammy he was, just like his mother! *"Croak, croak, croak!"* was all he could say when he saw the pretty little girl in the walnut shell.

"Don't talk so loud or you'll wake her," said the old toad. "She might escape us even now; she is as light as a feather. We will put her at once on a broad water lily in the stream. That will be quite an island for her, since she is so small and light. She can't run away from us there, whilst we are preparing the guest chamber under the marsh where she shall live."

In the brook grew many water lilies with broad, green leaves. They looked as if they were swimming about on the water. The lily farthest away was the largest, and it was to this one that the old toad swam with Thumbelina in her walnut shell.

The tiny Thumbelina woke up very early in the morning. When she saw where she was she began to cry bitterly; on every side of the great, green leaf was water, and she could not get to the land.

The old toad was down under the marsh, decorating a room with rushes and yellow marigold leaves, to make it very grand for her new daughter-in-law. Then she swam out with her ugly son to the leaf where Thumbelina lay. She wanted to fetch the pretty cradle to put it into the room before Thumbelina herself came there. In the water, the old toad bowed low before Thumbelina and said: "Here is my son; you shall marry him and live in great magnificence down under the marsh."

"Croak, croak, croak!" was all that the son could say. Then he and his mother took the neat little cradle and swam away with it.

The little fishes swimming about under the water had seen the toads quite plainly and heard what the mother had said, so they put their heads out of the water to see the little girl. When they saw her, they thought her so pretty that they were very sorry she should go down with the ugly toads to live. No, that must not happen. They assembled in the water round the green stalk that supported the leaf on which she was sitting, and they nibbled the stem in two. Away floated the leaf down the stream, bearing Thumbelina far beyond the reach of the toads.

A great beetle came flying past and caught sight of Thumbelina. In a moment he put his arms around her slender waist, flew off with her to the bank of the stream, and put her on a daisy.

The whole summer poor little Thumbelina lived alone in the great woods. She wove a bed for herself of blades of grass and hung it up under a clover leaf to protect herself from the rain. She gathered honey from the flowers for food, and she drank the dew on the leaves every morning.

Thus the summer and autumn passed, but then came the winter—the long, harsh winter. She was terribly cold, for her clothes were ragged and she herself was so small and thin. Poor little Thumbelina! She would surely freeze to death. And what was worse, it began to snow. To Thumbelina, every snowflake that fell on her was like a whole shovelful thrown on one of us, for we are so big and she was only an inch high.

Just outside the woods where she was living, she came across the door of a field mouse's hole under a cornstalk. There the mouse lived warm and snug, with a storeroom full of corn, a splendid kitchen, and a dining room. Poor little Thumbelina went up to the door and begged for a little piece of barley, for she had not had anything to eat for the last two days.

"Poor little creature!" said the field mouse, for she was a kind old thing at heart. "Come into my warm room and have some dinner with me." Gratefully, Thumbelina said yes.

As Thumbelina pleased her, the field mouse said, "As far as I am concerned, you may spend the winter with me. But you must keep my room clean and tidy, and tell me stories, for I like that very much."

Thumbelina did all that the kind old field mouse asked, and she did it remarkably well too.

"Now I am expecting a visitor," said the field mouse. "My neighbor comes to call on me once a week. He is better off than I am. He has great big rooms and wears a fine black velvet coat. He is so rich and accomplished," the field mouse went on, "that his house is twenty times larger than mine. If you could only marry him, you would be well provided for. But he is blind. Although he possesses great knowledge, he cannot bear being in the sun or around the beautiful flowers. In fact, he speaks harshly of them, for he has never seen them. You must tell him all the prettiest stories you know."

But Thumbelina did not trouble her head about him, for he was only a mole. He came and paid them a visit, wearing his black velvet coat.

Thumbelina had to sing to him, so she sang "Ladybird, Ladybird, Fly Away Home!" and other songs so prettily that the mole fell in love with her; but he did not say anything, for he was very cautious. A short time before, he had dug a long passage through the ground from his own house to that of his neighbor; he gave the field mouse and Thumbelina permission to walk in this tunnel as often as they liked. But he begged them not to be afraid of the dead bird that lay in the passage. He must have died a little time ago; now he lay buried just where the mole had made his tunnel.

The mole decided to show Thumbelina and the mouse the way through his tunnel. So, in his mouth he took a piece of rotten wood that glowed like fire in the dark. He went in front, lighting the way for them through the long, dark passage. When they came to the place where the dead bird lay, the mole put his broad nose against the ceiling and pushed a hole through, so that a little daylight could shine down. In the middle of the path lay the dead swallow, his pretty wings pressed close to his sides, his claws and head cold. Thumbelina was very sorry, for she was very fond of all little birds; they had sung and twittered so beautifully to her all through the summer. When the other two turned away she kissed the bird's closed eyes gently.

The mole closed up the hole that let in the light and then escorted the ladies home. But Thumbelina could not sleep that night, so she got out of bed, wove a great big blanket of straw, and carried it off to the mole's passage. She spread it over the dead bird, and upon it she piled thistledown as soft as cotton wool, which she had found in the field mouse's room. At least the poor little thing would lie warmly buried.

"Farewell, pretty little bird!" she said. "Farewell, and thank you for your beautiful songs in the summer, when the trees were green and the sun shone down warmly on us!" Then she laid her head against the bird's heart. But the bird was not dead—he had been frozen, and now that she had warmed him, he was coming to life again.

Thumbelina trembled. She was so frightened, for the bird was very large in comparison with herself, only an inch high. But she took courage and piled the down more thickly over the poor swallow. She even fetched her own coverlet and laid it over his head.

On the next night she crept out again to him. There he was, alive but very weak. He could only open his eyes for a moment and look at Thumbelina, who was standing in front of him with a piece of rotten wood in her hand, for she had no other lantern.

"Thank you, pretty little child!" said the swallow to her. "I am so beautifully warm! Soon I shall regain my strength, and then I shall be able to fly out again into the warm sunshine."

"Oh," said Thumbelina. "It is very cold outside; it is snowing and freezing! Stay in your warm bed. I will take care of you!"

Then she brought him water in a petal, which he drank. After this he related to her how he had torn one of his wings on a bramble, so that he could not fly as fast as the other swallows who had flown far away to warmer lands. Finally, exhausted, he had dropped, and then he could remember no more.

The whole winter the bird remained down there, and Thumbelina looked after him, nursing him tenderly. Neither the mole

" NOW HE CAN'T SING ! "

nor the field mouse learned anything of this, for they ignored the poor swallow.

When the spring came and the sun warmed the earth again, the swallow said farewell to Thumbelina, who opened the hole that the mole had made in the roof. The sun shone brightly down upon her, and the swallow asked her if she would go with him; she could sit upon his back. Thumbelina wanted very much to fly far into the green wood, but she knew that the old field mouse would be sad if she ran away. "No, I mustn't go!" she said.

"Farewell, dear good little girl!" said the swallow, and he flew off into the sunshine. Thumbelina gazed after him with tears in her eyes, for she was very fond of the swallow.

Thumbelina grew very unhappy without the swallow. The field mouse did not allow her to go out into the warm sunshine. Soon the corn that had been sowed in the field over the field mouse's home started to grow. It grew so high that it made a thick forest for the poor little girl, who was only an inch tall.

"Now you are to be a bride, Thumbelina," said the field mouse one day, "for our neighbor has asked for your hand! What a piece of fortune for a poor child like you! Now you must set to work at your linen for your dowry, for nothing must be lacking if you are to become the wife of our neighbor, the mole!"

But Thumbelina was not at all pleased about this, for she did not like the stupid mole. Every morning when the sun was rising and every evening when it was setting, she would steal out of the mouse's home. Then the breeze would part the ears of corn so that she could see the blue sky through them. She would think how bright and beautiful it must be outside, and she would long to see her dear swallow again. But he never came; no doubt he had flown away far into the great green woods.

By the autumn Thumbelina had finished her dowry.

"In four weeks you will be married!" said the field mouse. "Don't be obstinate, or I shall bite you with my sharp white teeth! You will get a fine husband! The king himself has not such a velvet coat. The mole's storeroom and cellar are full, and you should be thankful for that."

Well, the wedding day arrived. The mole had come to fetch Thumbelina to live with him deep down underground, never to come out into the warm sun again, for that was what he didn't like. The poor little girl was very sad, for now she must say good-bye to the beautiful sun.

"Farewell, bright sun!" she cried. And she stretched out her arms toward it, taking another step outside the house, for now the corn had been reaped and only the dry stubble was left standing. "Farewell, farewell!" she said, and she put her arms around a lit-tle red flower that grew there. "Give my love to the dear swallow when you see him!"

"Tweet, tweet!" sounded in her ear all at once. She looked up. There was the swallow flying past! As soon as he saw Thumbel-ina, he was very glad. She told him how unwilling she was to marry the ugly mole, as then she would have to live under-ground where the sun never shone. She could not help bursting into tears.

"The cold winter is coming now," said the swallow. "I must fly away to warmer lands. Will you come with me? You can sit on my back, and we will fly far away from the ugly mole and his dark house, over the mountains, to the warm countries where the sun shines more brightly than it does here. There it is always summer, and beautiful flowers are always growing. Do come with me, dear little Thumbelina who saved my life when I lay frozen in the dark tunnel!"

"Yes, I will go with you," said Thumbelina, and she got on the swallow's back, with her feet on one of his outstretched wings. Up he flew into the air, over woods and seas, over the great moun-tains where the snow is always lying. And whenever she was cold she crept under his warm feathers, keeping only her little head out to admire all the beautiful things in the world beneath. At last they came to warm lands, where the sun was brighter, the sky seemed twice as high, and in the hedges hung the finest green and purple grapes.

Under the most splendid green trees beside a blue lake stood a glittering white marble castle. Vines hung about the high pil-lars; among them were many swallows' nests, and in one of these lived the swallow who was carrying Thumbelina.

"Here is my house!" said he. "But it won't do for you to live with me; I am not tidy enough to please you. Find a home for yourself in one of the lovely flowers that grow down there. Now I will set you down, and you can do whatever you like."

"That will be splendid!" said she, clapping her little hands.

There lay a great white marble column that had fallen to the ground and broken into three pieces. Between these sections grew the most beautiful white flowers. The swallow flew down with Thumbelina and set her upon one of the broad leaves. But to her astonishment, sitting in the middle of the flower was a tiny man. He had the prettiest golden crown on his head and the most beautiful wings on his shoulders, and he was no bigger than Thumbelina. He was the spirit of the flower. In each blossom there dwelt a tiny man or woman; but this one was the king over the others.

"How handsome he is!" whispered Thumbelina to the swallow, shyly.

The little king was very much frightened of the swallow, for in comparison with one so tiny as himself, the swallow seemed a giant. But when the king saw Thumbelina, he was delighted, for she was the most beautiful girl he had ever seen. So he took his golden crown from his head and put it on hers, asking her name and if she would be his wife, becoming queen of all the flowers.

"Yes," thought Thumbelina, "he would certainly be a different kind of husband than the son of the toad or the mole with his black velvet coat." So she said yes to the noble king. And out of each flower came a lady and gentleman, each so tiny and pretty that it was a pleasure to see them. Each brought Thumbelina a wedding present. But the best gift of all was the beautiful pair of wings that the little king fastened onto her back. Now she too could fly from flower to flower. All wished the couple joy, and the swallow sat above in his nest and sang the wedding march as well as he could. But he was sad, because he was very fond of Thumbelina and did not want to be separated from her.

"You shall not be called Thumbelina!" said the king of the spirits to her. "That is an ugly name, and you are much too pretty for that. We will call you May Blossom."

"Farewell, farewell!" said the little swallow with a heavy heart, as he flew away.

When spring came, the swallow flew back north. There he had a little nest above the window of a small house. In this house lived a woman who told fairy stories. *"Tweet, tweet!"* the swallow sang to her. And that is the way we learned the whole story.

The Frog Prince

n the old times, when it was still of some use to wish for the thing one wanted, there lived a king whose daughters were all quite handsome. But the youngest was so beautiful that the sun himself, who has seen so much, wondered at her beauty each time he shone over her. Near the royal castle there was a great, dark forest, and in the forest under an old linden tree was a well. When the day was hot, the king's daughter used to go forth into the woods and sit by the brink of the cool well. If the time seemed long, she would take out a golden ball and throw it up and catch it again—this was her favorite pastime.

Now it happened one day that the golden ball, instead of falling back into the maiden's little hand that had sent it aloft, dropped near the edge of the well and rolled in. The king's daughter followed it with her eyes as it sank, but the well was deep, so deep that the bottom could not be seen. Then she began to weep, and she wept and wept as if she could never be comforted. And in the midst of her weeping she heard a voice say to her, "What ails thee, king's daughter? Thy tears would melt a heart of stone."

When she looked to see where the voice had come from, there was nothing but a frog stretching his thick, ugly head out of the water.

"Oh, is it you, old waddler?" said she. "I weep because my golden ball has fallen into the well."

"Never mind, do not weep," answered the frog. "I can help thee, but what wilt thou give me if I fetch up thy ball again?"

"Whatever you like, dear frog," said she. "Any of my clothes, my pearls and jewels, or even the golden crown that I wear."

"Thy clothes, thy pearls and jewels, and thy golden crown are not for me," answered the frog. "But if thou wouldst love me, have me for thy companion and playfellow, let me sit by thee at table, eat from thy plate, drink from thy cup, and sleep in thy little bed—if thou wouldst promise all this, then would I dive below the water and fetch thy golden ball again."

"Oh, yes," she answered. "I will promise it all, whatever you want, if you will only get me my ball again."

But she thought to herself, "What nonsense he talks! As if he could do anything but sit in the water and croak with the other frogs. How could he possibly be anyone's companion?"

But the frog, as soon as he heard her promise, drew his head under the water and sank down out of sight. After a while he came to the surface again with the ball in his mouth, and he threw it on the grass.

The king's daughter was overjoyed to see her pretty plaything again, and she caught it up and ran off with it.

"Stop! Stop!" cried the frog. "Take me up too! I cannot run as fast as you!"

But it was of no use, for croak after her as he might, she would not listen to him but made haste home. Very soon she forgot all about the poor frog, who had to return to his well again.

The next evening, when the king's daughter was sitting at table with the king and all the court, eating from her golden plate, something came pitter-patter up the marble stairs. Then there came a knocking at the door, and a voice cried out, "King's youngest daughter, let me in!"

And she got up and ran to see who it could be. But when she opened the door, there was the frog sitting outside. She shut the door hastily and went back to her seat, feeling very uneasy. The king noticed how quickly her heart was beating, and he said, "My child, what art thou afraid of? Is there a giant standing at the door ready to carry thee away?"

"Oh, no," answered she. "No giant, but a horrid frog."

"And what does the frog want?" asked the king.

"Oh, dear Father," answered she, "when I was sitting by the well yesterday and playing with my golden ball, it fell into the water. While I was crying for the loss of it, the frog came and got it again for me on condition I would let him be my companion. I never thought that he could leave the water and come after me, but now there he is outside the door, and he wants to come in to stay with me."

And then they all heard him knocking a second time and crying:

> "King's youngest daughter,
> Open to me!
> By the well water,
> What promised thou me?
> King's youngest daughter,
> Now open to me!"

"That which thou hast promised must thou perform," said the king, "so go now and let him in."

So she went and opened the door, and the frog hopped in, following at her heels till she reached her chair. Then he stopped and cried, "Lift me up to sit by thee."

But she delayed doing so until the king ordered her. Once the frog was on the chair, he climbed onto the table, and there he sat and said, "Now push thy golden plate a little nearer, so that we may eat together."

And so she did, but everybody could see how unwilling she was. Every morsel seemed to stick in her throat, while the frog feasted heartily.

"I have had enough now," said the frog at last, "and as I am tired, thou must carry me to thy room and make ready thy silken bed. Then we will lie down and go to sleep."

SHE WAS AFRAID OF THE COLD FROG

The king's daughter began to weep. She was afraid to let the cold frog sleep in her pretty, clean bed. She thought that nothing would satisfy him. Now the king grew angry with her, saying, "That which thou hast promised in thy time of necessity, must thou now perform."

So she picked up the frog with her finger and thumb, carried him upstairs, and put him in a corner. When she had lain down to sleep, he came creeping up, saying, "I am tired and want sleep as much as thou. Take me up into thy bed, or I will tell thy father."

Then she felt beside herself with rage and, picking him up, she threw him with all her strength against the wall, crying, "Now you will be quiet, you horrid frog!"

But as he fell, he ceased to be a frog and became all at once a prince with beautiful, kind eyes. And it came to pass that, with her father's consent, they became bride and bridegroom. And he told her how a wicked witch had bound him by her spells, and how no one but she alone could have released him. And there came to the door a carriage drawn by eight white horses with white plumes on their heads and golden harnesses. The prince and princess were carried away to his father's kingdom, where they lived happily thereafter.

The Elephant's Child

In the High and Far-Off Times the Elephant, O Best Beloved, had no trunk. He had only a blackish, bulgy nose, as big as a boot, that he could wriggle about from side to side; but he couldn't pick up things with it. But there was one Elephant—a new Elephant—an Elephant's Child—who was full of 'satiable curtiosity, and that means he asked ever so many questions. And he lived in Africa, and he filled all Africa with his 'satiable curtiosities. He asked his tall aunt, the Ostrich, why her tail feathers grew just so, and his tall aunt, the Ostrich, spanked him with her hard, hard claw. He asked his tall uncle, the Giraffe, what made his skin spotty, and his tall uncle, the Giraffe, spanked him with his hard, hard hoof. And still he was full of 'satiable curtiosity! He asked his broad aunt, the Hippopotamus, why her eyes were red, and his broad aunt, the Hippopotamus, spanked him with her broad, broad hoof. And he asked his hairy uncle, the Baboon, why melons tasted just so, and his hairy uncle, the Baboon, spanked him with his hairy, hairy paw. And *still* he was full of 'satiable curtiosity! He asked questions about everything that he saw, or heard, or felt, or smelt, or touched, and all his uncles and his aunts spanked him. And still he was full of 'satiable curtiosity!

One fine morning in the middle of the Precession of the

Equinoxes, this 'satiable Elephant's Child asked a new fine question that he had never asked before. He asked, "What does the Crocodile have for dinner?" Then everybody said, "Hush!" in a loud and dretful tone, and they spanked him immediately and directly, without stopping, for a long time.

By and by, when that was finished, he came upon the Kolo-kolo Bird sitting in the middle of a wait-a-bit thornbush, and he said, "My father has spanked me, and my mother has spanked me; all my aunts and uncles have spanked me for my 'satiable cur-tiosity; and *still* I want to know what the Crocodile has for din-ner!"

The Kolokolo Bird said, with a mournful cry, "Go to the banks of the great gray-green, greasy Limpopo River, all set about with fever-trees, and find out."

That very next morning, when there was nothing left of the Equinoxes, because the Precession had preceded according to precedent, this 'satiable Elephant's Child took a hundred pounds of bananas (the little, short, red kind), and a hundred pounds of sugarcane (the long, purple kind), and seventeen melons (the greeny-crackly kind), and said to all his dear families, "Good-bye. I am going to the great gray-green, greasy Limpopo River, all set about with fever-trees, to find out what the Crocodile has for din-ner." And they all spanked him once more for luck, though he asked them most politely to stop.

Then he went away, a little warm but not at all astonished, eating melons and throwing the rind about, because he could not pick it up.

He went from Graham's Town to Kimberley, and from Kim-berley to Khama's Country, and from Khama's Country he went east by north, eating melons all the time, till at last he came to the banks of the great gray-green, greasy Limpopo River, all set about with fever-trees, precisely as Kolokolo Bird had said.

Now you must know and understand, O Best Beloved, that till that very week, and day, and hour, and minute, this 'satia-ble Elephant's Child had never seen a Crocodile, and did not know what one was like. It was all his 'satiable curtiosity.

The first thing that he found was a Bi-Coloured-Python-Rock-

Snake curled round a rock.

" 'Scuse me," said the Elephant's Child most politely, "but have you seen such a thing as a Crocodile in these promiscuous parts?"

"*Have* I seen a Crocodile?" said the Bi-Coloured-Python-Rock-Snake, in a voice of dretful scorn. "What will you ask me next?"

" 'Scuse me," said the Elephant's Child, "but could you kindly tell me what he has for dinner?"

Then the Bi-Coloured-Python-Rock-Snake uncoiled himself very quickly from the rock and spanked the Elephant's Child with his scalesome, flailsome tail.

"That is odd," said the Elephant's Child, "because my father and my mother, and my uncle and my aunt, not to mention my other aunt, the Hippopotamus, and my other uncle, the Baboon, have all spanked me for my 'satiable curtiosity—and I suppose this is the same thing."

So he said good-bye very politely to the Bi-Coloured-Python-Rock-Snake, and helped to coil him up on the rock again, and went on, a little warm, but not at all astonished, eating melons, and throwing the rind about, because he could not pick it up, till he trod on what he thought was a log of wood at the very edge of the great gray-green, greasy Limpopo River, all set about with fever-trees.

But it was really the Crocodile, O Best Beloved, and the Crocodile winked one eye—like this!

" 'Scuse me," said the Elephant's Child most politely, "but do you happen to have seen a Crocodile in these promiscuous parts?"

Then the Crocodile winked the other eye, and lifted half his tail out of the mud; and the Elephant's Child stepped back most politely, because he did not wish to be spanked again.

"Come hither, Little One," said the Crocodile. "Why do you ask such things?"

" 'Scuse me," said the Elephant's Child most politely, "but my father has spanked me, my mother has spanked me, not to mention my tall aunt, the Ostrich, and my tall uncle, the Giraffe, who can kick ever so hard, as well as my broad aunt, the Hippopotamus, and my hairy uncle, the Baboon, *and* including the Bi-Coloured-Python-Rock-Snake, with the scalesome, flailsome tail, just

56

THE ELEPHANT'S CHILD

up the bank, who spanks harder than any of them; and *so*, if it's quite all the same to you, I don't want to be spanked anymore."

"Come hither, Little One," said the Crocodile, "for I am the Crocodile," and he wept crocodile-tears to show it was quite true.

Then the Elephant's Child grew all breathless, and panted, and kneeled down on the bank and said, "You are the very person I have been looking for all these long days. Will you please tell me what you have for dinner?"

"Come hither, Little One," said the Crocodile, "and I'll whisper to you."

Then the Elephant's Child put his head down close to the Crocodile's musky, tusky mouth, and the Crocodile caught him by his little nose, which up to that very week, day, hour, and minute, had been no bigger than a boot, though much more useful.

"I think," said the Crocodile—and he said it between his teeth, like this—"I think today I will begin with Elephant's Child!"

At this, O Best Beloved, the Elephant's Child was much annoyed, and he said, speaking through his nose, like this, "Led go! You are hurtig be!"

Then the Bi-Coloured-Python-Rock-Snake scuffled down from the bank and said, "My young friend, if you do not now, immediately and instantly, pull as hard as ever you can, it is my opinion that your acquaintance in the large-pattern leather ulster" (and by this he meant the Crocodile) "will jerk you into yonder limpid stream before you can say Jack Robinson."

This is the way Bi-Coloured-Python-Rock-Snakes always talk.

Then the Elephant's Child sat back on his little haunches, and pulled, and pulled, and pulled, and his nose began to stretch. And the Crocodile floundered into the water, making it all creamy with great sweeps of his tail, and *he* pulled, and pulled, and pulled.

And the Elephant's Child's nose kept on stretching; and the Elephant's Child spread all his little four legs and pulled, and pulled, and pulled, and his nose kept on stretching. And the Crocodile threshed his tail like an oar, and *he* pulled, and pulled, and pulled, and at each pull the Elephant's Child's nose grew longer and longer—and it hurt him hijjus!

Then the Elephant's Child felt his legs slipping, and he said through his nose, which was now nearly five feet long, "This is too butch for be!"

Then the Bi-Coloured-Python-Rock-Snake came down from the bank and knotted himself in a double clove hitch round the Elephant's Child's hind legs, and said, "Rash and inexperienced traveler, we will now seriously devote ourselves to a little high tension, because if we do not, it is my impression that yonder self-propelling man-of-war with the armour-plated upper deck" (and by this, O Best Beloved, he meant the Crocodile) "will permanently vitiate your future career."

That is the way all Bi-Coloured-Python-Rock-Snakes always talk.

So he pulled, and the Elephant's Child pulled, and the Crocodile pulled; but the Elephant's Child and the Bi-Coloured-Python-Rock-Snake pulled hardest, and at last the Crocodile let go of the Elephant's Child's nose with a plop that you could hear all up and down the Limpopo.

Then the Elephant's Child sat down most hard and sudden; but first he was careful to say thank you to the Bi-Coloured-Python-Rock-Snake; and next he was kind to his poor pulled nose, and wrapped it all up in cool banana leaves, and hung it in the great gray-green, greasy Limpopo to cool.

"What are you doing that for?" said the Bi-Coloured-Python-Rock-Snake.

" 'Scuse me," said the Elephant's Child, "but my nose is badly out of shape, and I am waiting for it to shrink."

"Then you will have to wait a long time," said the Bi-Coloured-Python-Rock-Snake. "Some people do not know what is good for them."

The Elephant's Child sat there for three days waiting for his nose to shrink. But it never grew any shorter, and besides, it made him squint. For, O Best Beloved, you will see and understand that the Crocodile had pulled it out into a really truly trunk same as all Elephants have today.

At the end of the third day a fly came and stung him on the shoulder, and before he knew what he was doing he lifted up his trunk and hit that fly dead with the end of it.

" 'Vantage number one!" said the Bi-Coloured-Python-Rock-Snake. "You couldn't have done that with a mere-smear nose. Try and eat a little now."

Before he thought what he was doing, the Elephant's Child put out his trunk and plucked a large bundle of grass, dusted it clean against his forelegs, and stuffed it into his own mouth.

" 'Vantage number two!" said the Bi-Coloured-Python-Rock-Snake. "You couldn't have done that with a mere-smear nose. Don't you think the sun is very hot here?"

"It is," said the Elephant's Child, and before he thought what he was doing, he schlooped up a schloop of mud from the banks of the great gray-green, greasy Limpopo and slapped it on his head, where it made a cool schloopy-sloshy mud-cap all trickly behind the ears.

" 'Vantage number three!" said the Bi-Coloured-Python-Rock-Snake. "You couldn't have done that with a mere-smear nose. Now how do you feel about being spanked again?"

" 'Scuse me," said the Elephant's Child, "but I should not like it at all."

"How would you like to spank somebody?" said the Bi-Coloured-Python-Rock-Snake.

"I should like it very much indeed," said the Elephant's Child.

"Well," said the Bi-Coloured-Python-Rock-Snake, "you will find that new nose of yours very useful to spank people with."

"Thank you," said the Elephant's Child. "I'll remember that; and now I think I'll go home to all my dear families and try."

So the Elephant's Child went home across Africa frisking and whisking his trunk. When he wanted fruit to eat he pulled fruit down from a tree, instead of waiting for it to fall as he used to do. When he wanted grass he plucked grass up from the ground, instead of going on his knees as he used to do. When the flies bit him he broke off the branch of a tree and used it as a fly whisk; and he made himself a new, cool, slushy-squshy mud-cap whenever the sun was hot. When he felt lonely walking through Africa he sang to himself down his trunk, and the noise was louder than several brass bands. He went especially out of his way to find a broad Hippopotamus (she was no relation of his), and he spanked her very hard, to make sure that the Bi-Coloured-Python-Rock-Snake had spoken the truth about his new trunk. The rest of the time he picked up the melon rinds that he had dropped on his way to the Limpopo—for he was a Tidy Pachyderm.

One dark evening he came back to all his dear families, and he coiled up his trunk and said, "How do you do?" They were very glad to see him, and immediately said, "Come here and be spanked for your 'satiable curtiosity."

"Pooh," said the Elephant's Child. "I don't think you peoples know anything about spanking; but *I* do, and I'll show you."

Then he uncurled his trunk and knocked two of his dear brothers head over heels.

"Oh Bananas!" said they. "Where did you learn that trick, and what have you done to your nose?"

"I got a new one from the Crocodile on the banks of the great gray-green, greasy Limpopo River," said the Elephant's Child. "I asked him what he had for dinner, and he gave me this to keep."

"It looks very ugly," said his hairy uncle, the Baboon.

"It does," said the Elephant's Child. "But it's very useful," and he picked up his hairy uncle, the Baboon, by one hairy leg, and hove him into a hornet's nest.

Then that bad Elephant's Child spanked all his dear families for a long time, till they were very warm and greatly astonished. He pulled out his tall Ostrich aunt's tail feathers; and he caught his tall uncle, the Giraffe, by the hind leg, and dragged him through the thornbush; and he shouted at his broad aunt, the Hippopotamus, and blew bubbles into her ear when she was sleeping in the water after meals; but he never let anyone touch the Kolokolo Bird.

At last things grew so exciting that his dear families went off one by one in a hurry to the banks of the great gray-green, greasy Limpopo River, all set about with fever-trees, to borrow new noses from the Crocodile. When they came back nobody spanked any-body anymore; and ever since that day, O Best Beloved, all the Elephants you will ever see, besides all those that you won't, have trunks precisely like the trunk of the 'satiable Elephant's Child.

The Six Swans

king was once hunting in the great woods, and he hunted the game so eagerly that none of his courtiers could follow him. When evening came on, he stood still and looked around him, and he saw that he had become quite lost. He sought a way out but could find none. Then he saw an old woman with a shaking head coming toward him. He didn't know she was a witch.

"Good woman," he said to her, "can you not show me the way out of the woods?"

"Oh, certainly, Sir King," she replied. "I can quite well do that, but on one condition, which you must fulfill or you will never get out of the woods, and will die of hunger."

"What is the condition?" asked the king.

"I have a daughter," said the old woman, "who is so beautiful that she has not her equal in the world, and she is well fitted to be your wife: if you will make her Lady Queen I will show you the way out of the woods."

In his anguish of mind, the king consented, and the old woman led him to her little house where her daughter was sitting by the fire. She received the king as if she were expecting him, and he saw that she was certainly very beautiful. But she did not please him, and he could not look at her without a secret feeling of horror. As soon as he had lifted the maiden onto his horse, the old woman showed him the way back to the palace. The king and his maiden arrived there safely, and soon the wedding was celebrated.

The king had already been married once, and he had by his first wife seven children—six boys and one girl—whom he loved more than anything in the world. And now, because he was afraid that their stepmother might not treat them well and might do them harm, he put them in a lonely castle that stood in the middle of the woods. It lay so hidden, and the way to it was so hard to find, that he himself could not have found it out had not a wise woman given him a reel of thread that possessed a marvelous property: when he threw it before him it unwound itself and showed him the way. But the king went so often to his dear children that the queen was offended by his absence. She grew curious and wanted to know what he had to do quite alone in the woods. She gave his servants a great deal of money, and they betrayed the secret to her, and also told her of the reel that alone could point the way. She did not rest till finally one day she found out where the king had been guarding the reel. Then she made some little white shirts and, as she had learned from her witch mother, sewed an enchantment into each of them.

And when the king had ridden off, she took the little shirts and went into the woods, and the reel showed her the way. The children, who saw someone coming in the distance, thought it was their dear father coming to them, and they sprang to meet him very joyfully. Then the queen threw over each child a little shirt. But when the shirts touched their bodies, the children were changed into swans, and they flew away over the forest. The queen went home quite satisfied, thinking she had gotten rid of her stepchildren. But the maiden had not run to meet the queen with her brothers, and neither the queen nor the sister knew of one another.

The next day the king came to visit his children, but he found no one but the maiden.

"Where are your brothers?" asked the king.

"Alas, dear father," she answered, "they have gone away and

THEY FLEW AWAY

left me all alone." And she told him that, looking out of her little windows, she had seen her brothers flying over the woods in the shape of swans. And she showed him the feathers she had collected, which they had let fall in the yard.

The king mourned, but he did not think that the queen had done the wicked deed. He was afraid to leave the maiden all alone in the woods. He wanted to take her back home with him. But she was afraid of the stepmother, and she begged the king to let her stay just one night more in the castle in the woods.

After the king had left his daughter, the poor maiden thought, "My home is no longer here; I will go and seek my brothers." And when night came she fled away into the forest.

She ran all through the night and the next day, till she could go no farther because of weariness. Then she saw a little hut, went in, and found a room with six little beds. She was afraid to lie down on one, so she crept under it, lying on the hard floor. She was going to spend the night there. But when the sun had set she heard a noise and saw six swans flying in through the window. They stood on the floor and blew at one another, blowing all their feathers off. Then each of their swan skins came off like a shirt. The maiden recognized her brothers, and she crept out from under the bed, overjoyed. Her brothers were not any less delighted to see their little sister again, but their joy did not last long.

"You cannot stay here," they said to her. "This is a den of robbers; if they were to come here and find you, they would kill you."

"Could you not protect me?" asked the little sister.

"No," they answered, "for we can only lay aside our swan skins for a quarter of an hour every evening. Only at this time do we regain our human forms, and then we are changed into swans again."

Then the little sister cried and said, "Is there not some way that I can free you?"

"Oh no," they said. "The conditions are too hard. You must not speak or laugh for six years, and must make in that time six shirts for us out of star flowers. If a single word comes out of your mouth, all your labor is in vain." And when the brothers said this, the quarter of an hour came to an end and they flew away out of the window as swans.

But the maiden had determined to free her brothers even if it should cost her her life. She left the hut, went into the forest, climbed a tree, and spent the night there. The next morning she went out, collected star flowers, and began to sew. She spoke to no one and she had no wish to laugh, so she sat there looking only at her work.

When she had lived there some time, it happened that the king of another country was hunting in the forest, and his hunters came to the tree on which the maiden sat. They called to her and said, "Who are you?"

But she gave no answer.

"Come down to us," they said. "We will do you no harm."

But she shook her head silently. The huntsmen would not leave her alone. They climbed the tree, lifted the maiden down, and led her to the king.

The king asked, "Who are you? What are you doing up that tree?" But she answered nothing.

He asked her in all the languages he knew, but she remained as dumb as a fish. Because she was so beautiful, however, the king's heart was touched, and he was seized with a great love for her. He wrapped her up in his cloak, placed her before him on his horse, and brought her to his castle. There he had her dressed in rich clothes, and her beauty shone out as bright as day. But still, not a word could be drawn from her. He set her at table by his side, and her modest ways and behavior pleased him so much that he said, "I will marry this maiden and none other in the world."

After some time, he married her. But the king had a wicked mother who was displeased with the marriage, and she said wicked things of the young queen. "Who knows who this girl is?" she said. "She cannot speak and is not worthy of a king."

After a year, when the queen had her first child, the old mother took him away from her. Then the old mother went to the king and said that the queen had killed the child. He would not believe it and would not allow any harm to be done to the queen.

So she sat quietly, sewing at the shirts and troubling herself about nothing. The next time she had a child, the wicked mother did the same thing, but again the king could not make up his mind to believe his mother. He said, "She is too sweet and good to do such a thing as that. If she were not dumb and could defend herself, her innocence would be proved." But when the third child was taken away, and the queen was again accused and could not utter a word in her own defense, the king was obliged to give her over to the law, which decreed that she must be burned to death. When the day came on which the sentence was to be executed, it was the last day of the six years in which the queen must not speak or laugh—and by doing so, she had finally freed her dear brothers from the power of the enchantment. The six shirts were almost done; all that remained to be sewn on was the left sleeve of the last shirt.

When she was led to the stake she laid the shirts on her arm, and as she stood on the pile and the fire was about to be lighted, she looked around her and saw six swans flying through the air. Then she knew that her release was at hand, and her heart danced for joy. The swans fluttered round her and hovered low so that she could throw the shirts over them. When they touched them the swan skins fell off, and her brothers stood before her— alive, well, and beautiful. Only the youngest had a swan's wing instead of his left arm, because his sister had not had enough time to finish his shirt. They embraced and kissed each other, and the queen went to the king, who was standing by in great astonishment, and said to him, "Dearest husband, now I can speak and tell you openly that I am innocent and have been falsely accused."

She told him of the old woman's deceit, and how she had taken the three children away and hidden them. Then they were brought back to the court, to the great joy of the king, and the wicked mother was banished from the country.

But the king and queen, with her six brothers, lived many years in happiness and peace.

The Nightingale

n China, as you know, the emperor is
Chinese and all his courtiers are also
Chinese. The story I am going to tell you
happened many years ago, but it is worth-
while for you to listen to it before it
is forgotten.

The emperor's palace was the most
splendid in the world, all made of price-
less porcelain but so brittle and delicate that you had to take
great care how you touched it. In the garden were the most beautiful flowers, and on the loveliest of them were tied silver bells
that tinkled. Everything in the emperor's garden was admirably
arranged, and it was so large that even the gardener himself did
not know where it ended. If you ever got beyond it, you came to
a stately forest that had great trees and deep lakes. The forest
sloped down to the sea, which was a clear blue. Large ships could
sail under the boughs of the trees, and in these trees there lived
a nightingale. She sang so beautifully that even the poor fisher-
man who had so much to do stood and listened when he came at
night to cast his nets.

From all the countries around came travelers to the emper-
or's town, and they were astonished at the palace and the garden. But when they heard the nightingale they all said, "This is
the finest thing of all!"

The travelers told all about it when they went home, and learned scholars wrote many books about the town, the palace, and the garden. But they did not forget the nightingale. She was praised the most, and all the poets composed splendid verses about her singing in the forest by the deep sea.

The books were circulated throughout the world, and some of them reached the emperor. He sat in his golden chair and read and read. He nodded his head every moment, for he liked reading the brilliant accounts of the town, the palace, and the garden. "But the nightingale is better than all," he saw written.

"What is that?" said the emperor. "I don't know anything about the nightingale! Is there such a bird in my empire, and so near as in my garden? I have never heard her! Fancy reading for the first time about her in a book!"

And he called his first lord to him and showed him the books. "Here is a most remarkable bird that is called a nightingale!" said the emperor. "They say she is the most glorious thing in my kingdom. Why has no one ever said anything to me about her?"

"I have never before heard her mentioned!" said the first lord. "I will look for her and find her!"

But where was she to be found? The first lord ran up and down stairs, through the halls and corridors; but none of those he met had ever heard of the nightingale. So the first lord ran again to the emperor and told him that she must be an invention on the part of those who had written the books.

"But the book in which I read this," said the emperor, "is sent me by His Great Majesty, the Emperor of Japan; so it cannot be untrue, and I will hear the nightingale! She must be here this evening! If she does not appear, the whole court shall be trampled underfoot after supper!"

"*Tsing pe!*" said the first lord; and he ran up and down stairs, through the halls and corridors. Half the court ran with him, for they did not want to be trampled underfoot. Everyone was asking after the wonderful nightingale, which all the world knew of, except those at court.

At last they met a poor little girl in the kitchen, who said,

"Oh! I know the nightingale well. How she sings! I have permission to carry the scraps over from the court meals to my poor sick mother, and when I am going home at night, tired and weary, I rest for a little in the woods. Then I hear the nightingale singing! It brings tears to my eyes, and I feel as if my mother were kissing me!"

"Little kitchen maid!" said the first lord. "I will give you a permanent place in the kitchen, and you shall have permission to see the emperor at dinner if you can lead us to the nightingale, for she is invited to come to court this evening."

And so they all went into the wood where the nightingale was wont to sing, and half the court went too. When they were on the way they heard a cow mooing.

"Oh!" said the courtiers, "now we have found her! What a wonderful power for such a small beast to have! I am sure we have heard her before!"

"No, that is a cow mooing!" said the little kitchen maid. "We are still a long way off!"

The frogs began to croak in the marsh. "Splendid!" said the Chinese chaplain. "Now we hear her; she sounds like a little temple bell!"

"No, no, those are frogs!" said the little kitchen maid. "But I think we shall soon hear her!"

Then the nightingale began to sing.

"There she is!" cried the little girl. "Listen! She is sitting there!" And she pointed to a little dark-gray bird up in the branches.

"Is it possible?" said the first lord. "I should never have thought it! How ordinary she looks! She must surely have lost her feathers."

"Little nightingale," called out the kitchen maid. "Our gracious emperor wants you to sing before him!"

"With the greatest of pleasure!" said the nightingale. So off to the palace they all went.

At the palace everything was splendidly prepared. In the center of the great hall where the emperor sat, there was a golden perch, on which the nightingale was placed. The whole court was there, and the little kitchen maid was allowed to stand behind the door.

The nightingale sang so gloriously that tears came into the emperor's eyes and ran down his cheeks. Then the nightingale sang even more beautifully, and her song went straight to all hearts. The emperor was so delighted that he said she should wear his gold slipper round her neck. But the nightingale thanked him and said she had had enough reward already. "I have seen tears in the emperor's eyes—that is a great reward. An emperor's tears have such power!" Then she sang again with her gloriously sweet voice.

She had to stay at court now. She was given her own cage, permission to walk out twice in the day and once at night, and twelve servants, each of whom held a silken string that was fastened round her leg. There was little pleasure in flying about like this.

One day the emperor received a large parcel on which was written "The nightingale."

"Here is another new book about our famous bird!" said the emperor.

But it was not a book. Instead, it was a little mechanical toy that lay in a box—an artifical nightingale that was like the real one, only it was set all over with diamonds, rubies, and sapphires. When it was wound up, it sang the same music as the real bird, moving its tail up and down, as it glittered with silver and gold. Round its neck was a little collar on which was written, "The nightingale of the emperor of Japan is nothing compared to that of the emperor of China."

"This is magnificent!" they all said, and the man who had brought the clockwork bird received, on the spot, the title of Bringer of the Imperial First Nightingale.

"Now they must sing together. What a duet we shall have!"

And so they sang together, but their voices did not blend, for the real nightingale sang in her own style and could not keep time with the clockwork bird who sang in a strict rhythm.

"It is not the artificial bird's fault!" said the bandmaster. "It

I WILL
SING
YOU A
LULLA
~BY

TROY · ALLYN · HOWELL

keeps very good time and is quite after my style!"

The artificial bird had to sing alone. It gave just as much pleasure as the real one, and it was so much prettier to look at; it sparkled like bracelets and necklaces. Three-and-thirty times it sang the same piece without being tired. People would like to have heard it again, but the emperor thought that the living nightingale should sing now—but where was she? No one had noticed that she had flown out the open window and away to her green woods.

"What shall we do?" asked the emperor.

And all the court scolded the nightingale and said that she was very ungrateful. "But we have still the best bird!" they said, and the artificial bird had to sing again, and that was the thirty-fourth time they had heard the same piece.

The real nightingale was banished from the kingdom.

The artificial bird was put by the emperor's bed on silken cushions, surrounded by all the gold and precious stones it had received as presents. And it was given the title of Imperial Night-Singer, First from the Left, for the emperor counted that side as the more distinguished, being the side on which the heart is.

So a whole year passed. The emperor, the court, and all the Chinese people knew every note of the artificial bird's song by heart.

But one evening, when the artificial bird was singing its best, and the emperor lay in bed listening to it, something in the bird went *crack*. Something had snapped! *Whir-r-r!* All the wheels ran down and then the music ceased. The emperor sprang up and had his physician summoned, but what could he do? Then the clock maker came, and after a great deal of talking and examining he put the bird somewhat in order. But he said that it must be very seldom used as its internal works were nearly worn out and it was impossible to put in new ones.

Here was a calamity! Only once a year was the artificial bird allowed to sing, and even that was almost too much for it. But each year the bandmaster made a little speech full of hard words, saying that it was just as good as before. So five years passed, and then a great sorrow came to the nation. The emperor, whom the

Chinese people loved and respected above all, was now ill, and it was said he was not likely to live.

Already a new emperor had been chosen, and the people stood outside in the street and asked the first lord how the old emperor was. The lord only shook his head.

Cold and pale lay the emperor in his splendid bed. The whole court believed him dead, and one after the other left him to pay their respects to the new emperor. Everywhere in the halls and corridors, cloth was laid down so that no footstep could be heard. Everything was still—very, very still—and nothing came to break the silence.

The emperor longed for something to come and relieve the monotony of this deathlike stillness. If only someone would speak to him! If only someone would sing to him! Music would carry his thoughts away and would break the spell lying on him. The moon was streaming in at the open window; but that too was silent, quite silent.

"Music! music!" cried the emperor feebly to the artifical bird. "You little bright golden bird, sing! Do sing! I gave you gold and jewels; I have hung my gold slipper around your neck with my own hands—sing! Do sing!" But the bird was silent. There was no one to wind it up, and so it could not sing. And all was silent, so terribly silent!

All at once there came in at the window the most glorious burst of song. It was the little living nightingale who, sitting outside on a bough, had heard the cry of her emperor and had come to sing to him of comfort and hope. And as she sang, the blood flowed quicker and quicker in the emperor's weak limbs, and life began to return.

"Thank you, thank you!" said the emperor. "You divine little bird! I know you. I chased you from my kingdom, but you have given me life again! How can I reward you?"

"You have done that already!" said the nightingale. "I brought tears to your eyes the first time I sang. I shall never forget that. They are jewels that rejoice a singer's heart. But now sleep and get strong again; I will sing you a lullaby." And the emperor fell into a deep, calm sleep as she sang.

The sun was shining through the window when he awoke, strong and well. None of his servants had come back yet, for they thought he was dead. But the nightingale sat and sang to him.

"You must always stay with me!" said the emperor. "You shall sing whenever you like, and I will break the artificial bird into a thousand pieces."

"Don't do that!" said the nightingale. "He did his work as long as he could. Keep him as you have done! I cannot build my nest in the palace and live here, but let me come whenever I like. I will sit in the evening on the bough outside the window, and I will sing you something that will make you feel happy and grateful. I will sing of joy and of sorrow; I will sing of the evil and the good which lies hidden from you. I love your heart more than your crown. Now I will sing to you again; but you must promise me one thing."

"Anything!" said the emperor, now standing up in his imperial robes.

"One thing I beg of you! Don't tell anyone that you have a little bird who tells you everything. It will be much better not to!" Then the nightingale flew away.

The servants came in to look at their dead emperor. But they were amazed and happy when the emperor said, "Good morning!"

Puss in Boots

here was a miller who, when he died, left no more estate to his three sons than his mill, his ass, and his cat. The eldest had the mill, the second the ass, and the youngest nothing but the cat.

The poor young fellow was quite comfortless at having so poor a lot. "My brothers," said he, "may get their living handsomely enough by joining their possessions together. But, for my part, when I have eaten up my cat and made me a muff of his skin, I must die of hunger."

Monsieur Puss, the cat, heard all this but made as if he did not. He said to the son with a grave and serious air, "Do not thus worry, my good master. You have nothing else to do but give me a bag and have a pair of boots made for me, so that I may scamper through the dirt and the brambles. Then you shall see that you have not so bad a portion as you imagine."

The puss's master did not build very much upon what the cat said. He had, however, often seen him play a great many cunning tricks to catch rats and mice (as when he used to hang by his heels, or hide himself in the meal, making as if he were dead). So he thought it wise to allow Puss to try to alter his miserable condition. When Puss had what he'd asked for, he gallantly put his boots on his feet and his bag about his neck. And with the strings of the bag in his two forepaws, he went into a warren where was great abundance of rabbits. He put bran and sow thistle into his bag and stretched out at length, as if he were dead. There he waited for some young rabbits not yet acquainted with the wicked ways of the world to come and rummage his bag for what he had put into it.

No sooner had he lain down than he had what he wanted: a rash and foolish young rabbit jumped into his bag, and Monsieur Puss, immediately drawing close the strings, took and killed him without pity. Proud of his prey, he went with it to the palace and asked to speak with His Majesty. He was shown upstairs into the king's apartment. Bowing low, he said to him, "I have brought you, sir, a rabbit of the warren, which my noble Lord, the Marquis of Carabas" (for that was the title that Puss was pleased to give his master) "has commanded me to present to Your Majesty from him."

"Tell thy master," said the king, "that I thank him, and that he does me a great deal of pleasure."

Another time Puss hid himself among some standing corn, holding his bag open. And when two partridges ran into it, he drew the strings and so caught them both. He went and made a present of these to the king, as he had done before with the rabbit that he had caught in the warren. The king, in like manner, received the partridges with great pleasure, and even gave him some money.

For two or three months Puss continued to carry to His Majesty, from time to time, game that he caught in his bag.

One day in particular, Puss discovered that the king was to ride in his coach along the river with his daughter, the most beautiful princess in the world. So Puss said to his master, "If you will follow my advice, your fortune is made. You have nothing else to do but go and wash yourself in the river, in that part I shall show you, and leave the rest to me."

The Marquis of Carabas did what Puss advised, without knowing why or wherefore. While he was washing, the king passed by, and Puss cried out, "Help! Help! My Lord, the Marquis of Carabas, is drowning!"

At this noise, the king put his head out of the coach window and, seeing the cat who had so often brought him such good game, he commanded his guards to run immediately to the assistance of His Lordship, the Marquis of Carabas. While they were drawing the poor marquis out of the river, Puss came up to the coach. He told the king that while his master was washing, there came by some rogues, who went off with his clothes. And the robbers had not been caught, even though his master had cried out "Thieves! Thieves!" several times, as loud as he could.

This cunning cat had hidden the clothes under a great stone. The king immediately commanded the officers of his wardrobe to run and fetch one of his best suits for the Marquis of Carabas.

The fine clothes the king gave the Marquis of Carabas set off the marquis's good looks, for he was well made and very handsome. The king's daughter took a secret inclination to him, and the Marquis of Carabas had no sooner cast two or three respectful and somewhat tender glances than she fell madly in love with him. The king requested that the marquis come into the coach and join them in their ride.

Puss, quite overjoyed to see his project begin to succeed, marched on ahead of the coach. He came upon some countrymen who were mowing a meadow, and he said to them, "Good people, you who are mowing, if you do not tell the king that the meadow you mow belongs to my Lord, the Marquis of Carabas, you shall be chopped as small as herbs for the pot."

The king did not fail to ask the mowers to whom the meadow they were mowing belonged.

"To my Lord, the Marquis of Carabas," answered they all together, for Puss's threats had made them terribly afraid.

"You see, sir," said the marquis, "this is a meadow which never fails to yield a plentiful harvest every year."

Puss, who went on still ahead of the coach, met with some reapers and said to them, "Good people, you who are reaping, if you do not tell the king that all this corn belongs to the Marquis of Carabas, you shall be chopped as small as herbs for the pot."

The king, who passed by a moment after, asked to whom all that corn did belong.

PUSS · IN · BOOTS

"To my Lord, the Marquis of Carabas," replied the reapers, and the king was very well pleased with it, as well as with the marquis, whom he congratulated thereupon. The cat, who went always ahead of the coach, said the same words to all he met, and the king was astonished at the vast estates of the Marquis of Carabas.

Monsieur Puss came at last to a stately castle, the master of which was an ogre who was the richest being the world had known (truly, all the lands that the king had just gone over belonged to this ogre). Puss, who had taken care to inform himself who this ogre was and what he was capable of doing, asked to speak with him, saying he could not pass so near the castle without having the honor of paying his respects to the ogre.

The ogre received him as politely as an ogre could do, and he made him sit down.

"I have been assured," said Puss, "that you have the gift of being able to change yourself into any sort of creature you have a mind to. You can, for example, transform yourself into a lion, an elephant, and the like."

"That is true," answered the ogre very briskly, "and to convince you, you shall see me now become a lion."

Puss was so terrified at the sight of a lion near him that he immediately got into the gutter because of his boots, which were of no use at all to him in walking upon the tiles. A little while after, when Puss saw that the ogre had resumed his natural form, he came down and admitted he had been very much frightened.

"I have been moreover informed," said Puss, "but I know not how to believe it, that you have also the power to take on you the shape of the smallest animals; for example, that you can change yourself into a rat or a mouse. But I must own to you I take this to be impossible."

"Impossible?" cried the ogre. "You shall see to that presently."

And at the same time he changed himself into a mouse, and began to run about the floor. Puss no sooner perceived this than he fell upon him and ate him up.

Meanwhile, as the king passed this fine castle of the ogre's, he had a mind to go into it. Puss, who heard the noise of His Majesty's coach running over the drawbridge, ran out and said to the king, "Your Majesty is welcome to this castle of my Lord, the Marquis of Carabas."

"What! Marquis," cried the king, "does this castle also belong to you? There can be nothing finer than this court and all the stately buildings that surround it. Let us go into it, if you please."

The marquis gave his hand to the princess and followed the king, who went first. They passed into a spacious hall, where they found the magnificent supper that the ogre had prepared for his friends (who dared not enter the castle now, knowing the king was there). His Majesty was perfectly charmed with the good qualities of the Marquis of Carabas, as was his daughter who, as we have seen, had fallen in love with him. Having seen the vast estate the marquis possessed, the king said to him, after having drunk five or six glasses of wine, "It will be owing to yourself only if you are not my son-in-law."

The marquis, making several low bows, accepted the honor that His Majesty had offered him, and forthwith, that very next day, he married the princess.

Puss became a great lord, and he never ran after mice anymore, except for sport.

The Glass Mountain

nce upon a time there was a glass mountain, at the top of which stood a castle made of pure gold, and in front of the castle there grew an apple tree on which there were golden apples.

Anyone who picked an apple gained admittance into the golden castle, and there in a silver room sat an enchanted princess of surpassing fairness and beauty. And she was as rich as she was beautiful, for the cellars of the castle were full of precious stones, and great chests of the finest gold stood round the walls of all the rooms.

Many knights had come from afar to try their luck, but it was in vain that they attempted to climb the mountain. In spite of having their horses shod with sharp nails, no one managed to get more than halfway up—they all fell back right down to the bottom of the steep, slippery glass hill. Sometimes one would break an arm, sometimes a leg, and many a brave man had even lost their lives.

The enchanted princess sat at her window and watched the bold knights trying to reach her on their splendid horses. The sight of her always gave men fresh courage, and they flocked from all corners of the globe to attempt the work of rescuing her. But it was all in vain, and for almost seven years the princess sat and waited for someone to scale the glass mountain.

A heap of corpses, both of riders and horses, lay round the mountain. And many dying men lay groaning there, unable to go any farther with their wounded limbs. The whole neighborhood had the appearance of a vast battlefield. Only three days before the end of the seventh year, a knight in golden armor, mounted on a spirited steed, was seen making his way toward the fatal hill.

Sticking his spurs into his horse, he made a rush at the mountain and got up halfway. Then he calmly turned his horse's head and came down again without a slip or stumble. The following day he started in the same way; the horse trod on the glass as if it were level earth, and sparks of fire flew from its hooves. All the other knights gazed in astonishment, for he almost gained the summit. In another moment he would have reached the apple tree, but all of a sudden a huge eagle rose up and spread its mighty wings, hitting the knight's horse in the eye. The beast shied, opened its wide nostrils, and tossed its mane. Then it reared high up in the air, its hind feet slipped, and it fell with its rider down the steep mountainside.

And then there was only one more day before the princess would have waited seven years. There arrived on the scene a mere schoolboy—a merry, happy-hearted youth who was, at the same time, strong and well grown. He saw how many knights had lost their lives in vain, but undaunted he approached the steep mountain on foot and began the ascent.

For a long time he had heard his parents speak of the beautiful princess who sat in the golden castle at the top of the glass mountain. He listened to all they said and determined that he too would try his luck. But first he took the sharp claws of a lynx and fastened them onto his own hands and feet.

Armed with these weapons, he boldly started up the glass mountain. The sun was going down, and the youth had not gotten more than halfway up. His feet were torn and bleeding, and he could only hold on now with his hands. As evening closed in, he strained his eyes to see if he could behold the top of the mountain. But then it suddenly became pitch-dark, and only the stars lit up the glass mountain. The poor boy still clung on as if glued

FOR ALL HIS STRENGTH HAD LEFT HIM

TROY·ALLYN·HOWELL

to the glass. He made no struggle to get higher, for all his strength had left him. Seeing no hope, he calmly awaited death. Then all of a sudden he fell into a deep sleep and, forgetful of his dangerous position, he slumbered sweetly. But all the same, although he slept, he had stuck his sharp claws so firmly into the glass that he was quite safe not to fall.

Now the golden apple tree was guarded by the eagle which had overthrown the golden knight and his horse. Every night it flew round the glass mountain keeping a careful lookout. So, no sooner had the moon emerged from the clouds than the bird rose up from the apple tree and, circling around in the air, it caught sight of the sleeping youth.

The bird swooped down and dug its sharp claws into the youth, who bore the pain without a sound, seizing the bird's two feet with his hands. The creature lifted him high up into the air and began to circle around the tower of the castle. The youth held on bravely. He saw the glittering palace, which by the pale rays of the moon looked like a dim lamp. Then he saw the high windows, and around one of them he spied a balcony in which the beautiful princess sat lost in sad thoughts.

When the boy saw that he was close to the apple tree, he drew a small knife from his belt and cut off one of the eagle's feet. The bird rose up into the air in its agony and vanished into the clouds, and the youth fell onto the broad branches of the apple tree.

He put peels from one of the golden apples on his wounds, and in one moment he was healed and well again. He picked several of the beautiful apples and put them in his pocket. Then he entered the castle. The door was guarded by a great dragon, but as soon as he threw an apple at it, the beast vanished.

At the same moment, a gate opened and the youth could see a courtyard full of flowers and beautiful trees, and on a balcony sat the lovely, enchanted princess.

As soon as she saw the youth, the princess ran toward him and greeted him as her husband and savior. She offered him all her treasures, and so the youth was now a rich and mighty ruler.

The next day, when the youth was strolling about in the palace garden with his wife, the princess, he looked down over the edge of the glass mountain and saw to his astonishment a great number of people gathered there. The princess blew her silver whistle, and the swallow who acted as messenger in the golden castle flew past.

"Fly down and ask what the matter is," the princess said to the little bird.

The messenger sped off like lightning and soon returned, saying, "The blood that fell from the eagle's wound has restored all the people below to life. All those who have perished on this mountain are awakening today, as if from a sleep. They are mounting their horses, and the whole population is gazing on this wonder with joy and amazement."

The Swineherd

here was once a poor prince who possessed a kingdom which, though small, was yet large enough for him to marry on, and married he wished to be.

Now it was certainly a little bold of him to say to the emperor's daughter, "Will you marry me?" But he did say so, for his name was known far and wide. There were hundreds of princesses who would gladly have said yes, but would the emperor's daughter say the same?

Well, we shall see.

On the grave of the prince's father grew a rose tree, a very beautiful rose tree. It only bloomed every five years, and then it bore but a single rose—but oh, such a rose! Its scent was so sweet that when you smelled it you forgot all your cares and troubles. The prince had also a nightingale that could sing as if all the beautiful melodies in the world were shut up in its little throat. The prince wanted the princess to have this rose and this nightingale, and so they were both put into silver caskets and sent to her.

The emperor had them brought to him in the great hall, where the princess was playing a song called "Here Comes a Duke A-riding" with her ladies-in-waiting. And when she caught sight of the big caskets that contained the presents, she clapped her hands for joy.

"If only it is a little pussycat!" she said. But the rose tree with the beautiful rose was taken out.

"But how prettily it is made!" said all the ladies-in-waiting.

"It is more than pretty," said the emperor. "It is charming!"

But the princess touched it, and then she almost began to cry.

"Ugh! Papa," she said, "it is not artificial; it is *real*!"

"Let us see first what is in the other casket before we begin to be angry," thought the emperor, and then out came the nightingale. It sang so beautifully that one could scarcely utter a cross word against it.

The emperor wept like a little child.

"Is this, at least, artificial?" asked the princess.

"No, it is a real bird," said those who had brought it.

"Then let the bird fly away," said the princess, and she would not on any account allow the prince to come.

But he was not daunted. He dirtied his face, drew his cap well over his eyes, and knocked at the door. "Good day, Emperor," he said. "Can I get a place here as servant in the castle?"

"Well," said the emperor, "there are so many who ask for a place that I don't know whether there will be one for you." Then he had a thought. "Stay," he said. "It has just occurred to me that I want someone to look after the swine, for I have so very many of them."

And so the prince got the position of Imperial Swineherd, and he had to live in a wretched little room close to the pigsties. The whole day he sat working, and when evening came he boiled tea in a pretty little pot he had made. All around it were little bells, and when the pot boiled they jingled most beautifully and played an old tune:

> "Where is Augustus dear?
> Alas! He's not here, here, here!"

Now the princess came walking past with all her ladies-in-waiting, and when she heard the tune she stood still and her face beamed with joy, for she also could play "Where Is Augustus Dear?"

"Why, that is what I play!" she said. "Listen! Go down and ask him what the instrument costs."

And one of the ladies-in-waiting had to go down to the swineherd's room near the pigsties. "What will you take for the pot?" asked the lady-in-waiting.

"I will have ten kisses from the princess," answered the swineherd.

"Heaven forbid!" said the lady-in-waiting.

"Yes, I will sell it for nothing less," replied the swineherd.

"Well, what does he say?" asked the princess.

"I hardly like to tell you," answered the lady-in-waiting.

"Oh, then you can whisper it to me."

So the lady-in-waiting did just that. "He is ill-mannered!" said the princess, and she went away. But she had only gone a few steps when the bells rang out so prettily:

"Where is Augustus dear?
Alas! He's not here, here, here."

"Listen!" said the princess. "Ask him whether he will take ten kisses from my ladies-in-waiting."

When he was asked, the swineherd said, "No, thank you. Ten kisses from the princess, or else I keep my pot."

Again the princess was told of his reply. "That is very tiresome!" said the princess. "Alas, I suppose if I am to have his pot, I must do as he says. But you must all put yourselves around me, so that no one else can see."

And together the ladies-in-waiting went down to the swineherd's room, placed themselves around the princess, and spread out their dresses to conceal her. Then the swineherd got his ten kisses, and the princess got the pot.

The swineherd—that is to say, the prince (though no one knew he was anything but a true swineherd)—let no day pass without making something. One day he made a rattle which, when it was turned round, played all the waltzes and polkas which had ever been known since the world began.

"That is superb!" said the princess as she passed by. "I have never heard a more beautiful composition. Listen! Go down and ask him what this instrument costs; but I won't kiss him again."

"He wants a hundred kisses from the princess," said the lady-in-waiting who had gone down to ask him.

"I believe he is mad!" said the princess, and then she went on. But she had only gone a few steps when she stopped.

"One ought to encourage art," she said. "I am the emperor's daughter! Tell him he shall have, as before, ten kisses; the rest he can take from my ladies-in-waiting."

"But we don't at all like being kissed by him," said the ladies-in-waiting.

"That's nonsense," said the princess. "If I can kiss him, you can too. Besides, remember that I give you board and lodging."

So the ladies-in-waiting had to go down to him again.

"A hundred kisses from the princess," said he. "Nothing more or less."

The ladies-in-waiting returned again with the swineherd's reply.

"Put yourselves around me once again," the princess said. So they all went once more to visit the swineherd, and the ladies-in-waiting put themselves around the princess, whom the swineherd began to kiss.

"What can that commotion be by the pigsties?" asked the emperor, who was standing on the balcony. He rubbed his eyes and put on his spectacles. "Why, those are the ladies-in-waiting playing their games; I must go down to them."

So he put on his slippers, which were once shoes though he had trodden them down into slippers. What a hurry he was in, to be sure!

As soon as he came into the yard he walked very softly, and the ladies-in-waiting were so busy counting the kisses that they never noticed the emperor. He stood on tiptoe.

"What is this?" he said when he saw the kissing; and then he threw one of his slippers at their heads just as the swineherd was

THE SWINEHERD

TROY·ALLYN·HOWELL

taking his eighty-sixth kiss.

"Be off with you!" said the emperor, for he was very angry. And he ordered the princess and the swineherd to be driven out of the empire.

Far away from home, the princess stood still and wept; the rain was streaming down, and all she had for company was the lowly swineherd.

"Alas, what an unhappy creature I am!" sobbed the princess. "If only I had taken the beautiful prince! Alas, how unfortunate I am!"

And the swineherd went behind a tree, washed his face, threw away his old clothes, and then stepped forward in his splendid dress, looking so beautiful that the princess was obliged to curtsy.

"It has come to this. I despise you!" he said. "You would have nothing to do with a noble prince. You did not understand the rose or the nightingale, but you could kiss the swineherd for the sake of a toy. This is what you get for it!" He went into his kingdom and shut the gate in her face, and she had to stay outside singing:

"Where's my Augustus dear?
Alas! He's not here, here, here!"

Toads and Diamonds

There was once upon a time a widow who had two daughters. The elder was so much like the widow, both in appearance and in nature, that whoever looked upon the daughter saw the mother. They were both so disagreeable and proud that there was no living with them.

The younger, who was the very picture of her father for courtesy and sweetness of temper, was also one of the most beautiful maidens ever seen. As people naturally love their own likeness, this mother doted upon her elder daughter. At the same time, she showed the greatest dislike for the younger, whom she kept at work continually and forced to eat in the kitchen.

Among other things, she made this poor child fetch water twice a day from a spring a mile and a half from the house, bringing home a pitcher full of it. One day as she was at the fountain, there came to her a poor woman, who begged of her to let her drink.

"Ay, with all my heart, good woman," said this pretty little girl. At once she rinsed the pitcher and took up some water at the clearest place of the fountain and gave it to her, holding up the pitcher all the while, that she might drink the easier.

The good woman, having drunk, said to her, "Thou art so

very pretty, my dear, and so good and mannerly that I cannot help giving thee a gift." For truly this woman was a fairy who had taken the form of a poor countrywoman to see how far the good manners of this pretty maiden would go. "I will give thee this gift," said the fairy, "that at every word thou speakest there shall come from thy mouth either a flower or a precious jewel."

When the little maiden came home her mother scolded her for staying so long at the fountain.

"I beg thee to pardon me, mother," said the poor girl, "for not making more haste." And as she spoke there came out of her mouth lovely roses, pearls, and diamonds.

"What can this be?" said her mother in amazement. "I really do believe that pearls and diamonds are falling from the girl's mouth! My dear! How can this be?"

Now this was the very first time she had called her "my dear."

Then the little maiden told her what had happened at the fountain in the forest; and all the time she spoke, numbers of diamonds and pearls kept on dropping from her mouth.

"This is wonderful!" cried her mother. "I must send thy sister there also. Fanny, Fanny, come here! Look what drops from thy sister's mouth when she speaks! Dear, wouldst not thou be glad to have the same gift bestowed on thee too? Thou hast nothing else to do but go and draw water from the fountain, and when a poor old woman appears and asks thee for a drink, to give it to her very politely."

"Oh," said this ill-bred minx, "it would be a very fine sight indeed to see *me* go draw water!"

"Go thou shalt, hussy," said her mother, "and this minute!"

And she had to go, grumbling all the way, taking with her the best silver tankard in the house.

She no sooner reached the fountain than she saw coming out of the woods a lady splendidly dressed, who came up to her and asked to drink. This, you must know, was the very fairy who had appeared to Fanny's sister, but she had now taken the form and dress of a beautiful princess, in order to see how far this girl's rudeness would go.

TOADS · AND · DIAMONDS

"Am I come hither, pray," said the proud, saucy daughter, "to serve thee with water? Dost thou think my fine silver tankard was brought for that? However, if thou hast a fancy, thou canst fill it thyself and drink."

"Thou art not over and above mannerly," said the fairy, without showing that she was at all angry. "Well, then, since thou hast so little breeding and art so rude, the gift I will bestow on thee is that at every word thou speakest there shall spring from thy mouth a snake or a toad." At this she vanished, and the girl went off home.

So soon as her mother saw her coming she cried out, "Well, daughter?"

"Well, mother?" answered the pert little hussy, and out of her mouth there jumped a viper and a toad.

"Mercy!" cried her mother. "What is this I see? Oh, it's that wretch, your sister, who has caused all this! But she shall pay for it!" And immediately seizing a stick, she ran to beat her. Hearing her angry words, the poor child fled from the house and hid herself among the trees in the forest.

At that moment the king's son, who was on his way home from hunting, rode by the spot where she was hiding. Noticing her among the bushes and seeing how beautiful she was, he asked her what she did there alone and why she was crying.

"Alas, sir," she answered, "my mother has driven me out of doors."

And as she spoke, the king's son, who had already fallen in love with her beauty, saw the pearls and the diamonds that dropped from her mouth. He desired her to tell him the whole story. When he had heard it, he lifted her onto his horse and took her with him to the palace of the king his father, and there he married her.

The Three Little Pigs

There was once upon a time a pig who lived with her three children on a large, comfortable, old-fashioned farmyard. The eldest of the little pigs was called Browny, the second Whitey, and the youngest and best-looking Blacky. Now Browny was a very dirty little pig, and I am sorry to say he spent most of his time rolling and wallowing about in the mud. He was never so happy as on a wet day, when the mud in the farmyard got soft and thick. Then he would steal away from his mother's side, find the muddiest place in the yard, and roll about in it, thoroughly enjoying himself. His mother would often find fault with him for this, but nothing could cure Browny of his bad habits.

Whitey was quite a clever little pig, but she was greedy. She was always thinking of her food and looking forward to her dinner. Whenever she saw the farmgirl carrying the pails across the yard, she would rise up on her hind legs and dance and caper with excitement. As soon as the food was poured into the trough, she jostled Blacky and Browny out of the way in her eagerness to get the best and biggest bits for herself. Her mother often scolded her for her selfishness, and she told her that some day she would suffer for being so greedy and grabbing.

Blacky was a good, nice little pig, neither dirty nor greedy.

He had dainty ways (for a pig), and his skin was always as smooth and shining as black satin.

Now, the time came when the mother pig felt old and feeble and near her end. One day she called the three little pigs to her and said, "My children, I feel that I am growing old and weak, and that I shall not live long. Before I die I should like to build a house for each of you, as this dear old sty in which we have lived so happily will be given to a new family of pigs, and you will have to leave. Now, Browny, what sort of a house would you like to have?"

"A house of mud," replied Browny, looking longingly at a wet puddle in the corner of the yard.

"And you, Whitey?" asked the mother pig.

"A house of cabbage," answered Whitey with a full mouth, scarcely raising her snout out of the trough in which she was grubbing for some potato parings.

"Foolish, foolish children!" said the mother pig, looking quite distressed. "And you, Blacky?" she asked, turning to her youngest son. "What sort of a house shall I order for you?"

"A house of brick please, Mother. This house will be warm in the winter, cool in summer, and safe all the year round."

"That is a sensible little pig," replied his mother, looking fondly at him. "I will see that the three houses are made ready at once. And now one last piece of advice. You have heard me talk of our old enemy, the fox. When he hears that I am dead, he is sure to try and get hold of you, to carry you off to his den. He is very sly and will no doubt disguise himself and pretend to be a friend, but you must promise me not to let him enter your houses on any pretext whatever."

A short time afterward the old mother pig died, and the little pigs went to live in their own houses. Browny was quite delighted with his soft mud walls and with the clay floor, which soon looked like nothing but a big mud pie. But that was what Browny enjoyed, and he was as happy as possible, rolling about all day and making a mess of himself. One day, as he was lying half-asleep in the mud, he heard a soft knock at his door, and a gentle voice said, "May I come in, Master Browny? I want to see your beautiful new house."

"Who are you?" said Browny, starting up in great fright, for though the voice sounded gentle, he felt sure it was a false voice, and he feared it was the fox.

"I am a friend come to call on you," answered the voice.

"No, no," replied Browny. "I don't believe you are a friend. You are the wicked fox, against whom our mother warned us. I won't let you in."

"O ho! is that the way you answer me?" said the fox, speaking very roughly in his natural voice. "We shall soon see who is master here," and with his paws he set to work and scraped a large hole in the soft mud walls. He quickly jumped through it, caught Browny, and trotted off with him to his den.

The next day, as Whitey was munching a few leaves of cabbage out of the corner of her house, the fox stole up to her door. He began speaking to her in the same gentle voice in which he had spoken to Browny, but it frightened her very much when he said, "I am a friend come to visit you, and to have some of your good cabbage for my dinner."

"Please don't touch it," cried Whitey in great distress. "The cabbages are the walls of my house, and if you eat them you will make a hole, and the wind and rain will come in and give me a cold." But it was too late, and in a minute the fox ate his way through the cabbage walls. He caught the trembling, shivering Whitey and carried her off to his den.

The next day the fox started off for Blacky's house, because he had made up his mind that he would get the three little pigs together in his den, kill them, and invite all his friends to a feast. But when he reached the brick house, he found that the door was bolted and barred, so in his sly manner he began, "Do let me in, dear Blacky. I have brought you a present of some eggs that I picked up in a farmyard on my way here."

"No, no, Mister Fox," replied Blacky, "I am not going to open my door to you. I know your cunning ways. You have carried off poor Browny and Whitey, but you are not going to get me."

This time the fox was so angry that he dashed with all his force against the wall and tried to knock it down. But it was too

"MAY I COME IN?"

TROY ALLYN HOWELL

strong and well built; and though the fox scraped and tore at the bricks with his paws, he only hurt himself. At last he had to give up and limp away, his forepaws all bleeding and sore.

"Never mind!" he cried angrily as he went off. "I'll catch you another day—see if I don't!—and won't I grind your bones to powder when I have got you in my den!" and he snarled fiercely, showing his teeth.

On the next day Blacky had to go into the neighboring town to do some marketing and buy a big kettle. As he was walking home with it slung over his shoulder, he heard a sound of steps stealthily creeping after him. For a moment his heart stood still with fear, and then a happy thought came to him. He had just reached the top of a hill and could see his own little house nestled at the foot of it among the trees. In a moment he snatched the lid off the kettle and jumped in himself. He lay quite snug in the bottom of the kettle, and with his foreleg he managed to put the lid on so that he was entirely hidden.

With a little kick from the inside he started the kettle off, and down the hill it rolled at full tilt. When the fox came up, all that he saw was a large, black kettle spinning over the ground at a great pace. Very much disappointed, he was just going to turn away, when he saw the kettle stop close to the little brick house. In a moment, Blacky jumped out and escaped with the kettle into the house. He barred and bolted the door and put the shutter up over the window.

"O ho!" exclaimed the fox to himself. "He thinks he will escape me that way, does he? We shall soon see about that, my friend," and very quietly and stealthily he prowled around the house, looking for some way to climb onto the roof.

In the meantime Blacky had filled the kettle with water, put it on the fire, and sat down quietly, waiting for it to boil. Just as the kettle was beginning to sing, and steam was coming out of the spout, he heard a sound like a soft, muffled step overhead—*patter, patter, patter*. The next moment he saw the fox's head and forepaws coming down the chimney. But Blacky very wisely took the lid off the kettle. With a yelp of pain, the fox fell into the boiling water. Before the fox could try to escape, Blacky popped the lid on, and the fox was scalded to death.

As soon as he was sure that their wicked enemy was really dead and could do them no further harm, Blacky started off to rescue Browny and Whitey. As he approached the den he heard piteous grunts and squeals from his poor little brother and sister. But when they saw Blacky appear at the entrance to the den, their joy knew no bounds. He quickly found a sharp stone and cut the cords by which they were tied to a stake in the ground, and then all three started off together for Blacky's house, where they lived happily ever after. From that day on, Browny quite gave up rolling in the mud, and Whitey ceased to be greedy, for they never forgot how nearly these faults had brought them to an untimely and painful end.

The Flying Ship

nce upon a time there lived an old couple who had three sons. The two elder were clever, but the third was a regular dunce. The clever sons were very fond of their mother, gave her good clothes, and always spoke pleasantly to her; but the youngest was always getting in her way, and she had no patience with him. Now, one day it was announced in the village that the king had issued a decree offering his daughter, the princess, in marriage to whomever should build a ship that could fly. Immediately the two elder brothers determined to try their luck and asked their parents' blessing. So the old mother smartened up their clothes and gave them a store of provisions for their journey. When they had gone the poor simpleton began to beg his mother to smarten him up and let him start off.

"What would become of a dolt like you?" she answered. "Why, you would be eaten up by wolves."

But the foolish youth kept repeating, "I will go, I will go, I will go!"

Seeing that she could do nothing with him, the mother gave him a crust of bread and a bottle of water, and she took no further heed of him.

So the simpleton set off on his way. When he had gone a short distance he met a little old dwarf. They greeted one another, and the dwarf asked him where he was going.

"I am off to the king's court," he answered. "He has promised to give his daughter to whomever can make a flying ship."

"And can you make such a ship?"

"Not I."

"Then why in the world are you going?"

"Can't tell," replied the simpleton.

"Well, if that is the case," said the dwarf, "sit down beside me. We can rest for a little while and have something to eat. Give me what you have got in your satchel."

Now, the poor simpleton was ashamed to show what was in it. However, he thought it best not to make a fuss, so he opened the satchel. He could scarcely believe his own eyes, for instead of the hard crust, he saw two beautiful fresh rolls and some cold meat. He shared them with the dwarf, who licked his lips and said, "Now, go into that wood and stop in front of the first tree. Then bow three times, strike the tree with your ax, fall to your knees on the ground with your face on the earth, and remain there. You may rise when you see there is a ship at your side. Step into it and fly to the king's palace. If you meet anyone on the way, take him with you."

The simpleton thanked the dwarf very kindly, bade him farewell, and went into the road. When he got to the first tree he stopped in front of it, did everything just as he had been told but, while kneeling on the ground with his face to the earth, he fell asleep. After a little time he awoke and, rubbing his eyes, he saw a ready-made ship at his side. At once he got into it. The ship rose and rose, and in a minute he was flying through the air. When the simpleton, who was on the lookout, looked down, he saw a man beneath him on the road. The man was kneeling with his ear upon the damp ground.

"Hello!" he called out. "What are you doing down there?"

"I am listening to what is going on in the world," replied the man lifting his head from the ground.

"Come with me in my ship," said the simpleton.

The man was only too glad to do so, and he got in beside the

simpleton. The ship flew and flew and flew through the air, till
again from his lookout the simpleton saw a man on the road below, who was hopping on one leg, while his other leg was tied up
behind his ear. So he hailed him, calling out, "Hello! What are you
doing, hopping on one leg?"

"I can't help it," replied the man. "I walk so fast that unless
I tie up one leg I should be at the end of the earth in a bound."

"Come with us on my ship," answered the simpleton. The
man made no objections and joined them, and the ship flew on and
on and on. Suddenly the simpleton, looking down on the road below, beheld a man aiming with a gun into the distance.

"Hello!" he shouted to him. "What are you aiming at? As far
as eye can see, there is no bird in sight."

"What would be the good of my taking a near shot?" replied
the man. "I can hit beast or bird at a hundred miles' distance.
That is the kind of shot I enjoy."

"Come with us in my ship," answered the simpleton. The
man made no objections and joined them, and the ship flew on and
on, farther and farther, till again the simpleton from his lookout
saw a man on the road below, carrying on his back a basket full
of bread. The simpleton waved to him and called out, "Hello!
where are you going?"

"To fetch bread for my breakfast."

"Bread? Why, you have a whole basket load of it on your
back."

"That's nothing," answered the man. "I should finish that in
one mouthful."

"Come along with us in my ship, then."

So the glutton joined the party, and the ship mounted again
into the air and flew up and onward. Soon the simpleton from his
lookout saw a man walking by the shore of a great lake, evi-
dently looking for something.

"Hello!" the simpleton cried to him. "What are you seeking?"

"I want water to drink, I'm so thirsty," replied the man.

"Well, there's a whole lake in front of you. Why don't you
drink some of that?"

"Do you call that enough?" answered the other. "Why, I

should drink it up in one gulp."

"Well, come with us in the ship."

And so the mighty drinker was added to the company, and the ship flew farther and even farther, till again the simpleton looked out. This time he saw beneath them a man dragging a bundle of wood while walking through the forest.

"Hello!" the simpleton shouted to him. "Why are you carrying wood through a forest?"

"This is not common wood," answered the other.

"What sort of wood is it, then?" asked the simpleton.

"If you throw it on the ground," said the man, "it will be changed into an army of soldiers."

"Come into the ship with us."

And so the man joined them; and away the ship flew on and on and on. Once more the simpleton looked out, and this time he saw a man carrying straw upon his back.

"Hello! Where are you carrying that straw to?"

"To the village," said the man.

"Do you mean to say that there is no straw in the village?"

"Ah, but this is quite peculiar straw. If you strew it about even in the hottest summer, the air at once becomes cold, the snow falls, and the people freeze."

Then the simpleton asked him also to join them.

At last the ship, with its strange crew, arrived at the king's court. The king was having his dinner, but he at once dispatched one of his courtiers to find out what the huge, strange new bird could be that had come flying through the air. The courtier peeped into the ship. Seeing what it was, he instantly went back to the king and told him that it was a flying ship, manned by a few peasants.

Then the king remembered his royal decree, but he made up his mind that he would never consent to let the princess marry a poor peasant. So he thought and thought, and then said to himself, "I will give him some impossible task to perform—that will be the best way to get rid of him." There and then, he decided to dispatch one of his courtiers to the simpleton, with the command that he was to fetch the king the healing water from the world's

THE SHIP FLEW ON AND ON

TROY·ALLYN·HOWELL

end before the king had finished his dinner.

But while the king was still instructing the courtier exactly what to say, the first man of the ship's company, the one with the miraculous power of hearing, had overheard the king's words and hastily reported them to the simpleton.

"Alas, alas!" cried the simpleton. "What am I to do now? It would take me quite a year, possibly my whole life, to find the water."

"Never fear," said the fleet-footed comrade. "I will fetch what the king wants."

Just then the courtier arrived, bearing the king's command.

"Tell His Majesty," said the simpleton, "that his orders shall be obeyed." And forthwith the swift runner unbound the foot that was strung up behind his ear and started off. In less than no time he had reached the world's end and drawn the healing water from the well.

"Dear me," he thought to himself, "that's rather tiring! I'll just rest for a few minutes; it will be some time yet before the king gets to dessert." So he threw himself down on the grass and, as the sun was very dazzling, he closed his eyes and fell sound asleep.

In the meantime all the ship's crew were anxiously awaiting him. Soon the king was about to finish dinner, and their comrade had not yet returned. So the man with the marvelous quick hearing lay down and, putting his ear to the ground, listened.

"That's a nice sort of fellow!" he suddenly exclaimed. "He's lying on the ground, snoring hard!"

At this the marksman seized his gun, took aim, and fired in the direction of the world's end, in order to awaken the sluggard. And a moment later the swift runner reappeared, stepped on board the ship, and handed the healing water to the simpleton. So while the king was still sitting at table finishing his dinner, news was brought to him that his orders had been obeyed to the letter.

What was to be done now? The king determined to think of a still more impossible task. So he told another courtier to go to the simpleton with the command that he and his comrades were instantly to eat up twelve oxen and twelve tons of bread. Once more the sharp-eared comrade overheard the king's words to the courtier, and he reported them to the simpleton.

"Alas, alas," sighed the simpleton. "What in the world shall I do? Why, it would take us a year, possibly our whole lives, to eat up twelve oxen and twelve tons of bread."

"Never fear," said the glutton. "It will scarcely be enough for me, I'm so hungry."

So when the courtier arrived with the royal message, he was told to take back word to the king that his orders would be obeyed. Then twelve roasted oxen and twelve tons of bread were brought alongside the ship, and at one sitting the glutton devoured it all.

"I call that a small meal," he said. "I wish they'd brought me some more."

Next, the king ordered that forty casks of wine, containing forty gallons each, were to be drunk up on the spot by the simpleton and his party. When these words were overheard by the sharp-eared comrade and repeated to the simpleton, the simpleton was in despair.

"Never fear," said his thirsty comrade. "I'll drink it all up at a gulp—see if I don't." Sure enough, when the forty casks of wine containing forty gallons each were brought alongside of the ship, they disappeared down the thirsty comrade's throat in no time. And when they were empty he remarked, "Why, I'm still thirsty. I would have been glad to have had two more casks."

Then the king took counsel with himself and sent an order to the simpleton that he would be wed to the princess only after having a bath, in a bathroom at the royal palace. Now, the bathroom was built of iron, and the king gave orders that it was to be heated to such a degree that it would suffocate the simpleton. So when the poor silly youth entered the room, he discovered that the iron walls were red-hot. But fortunately his comrade with the straw on his back had entered behind him. When the door was shut upon them he scattered the straw about, and suddenly the red-hot walls cooled down. Soon it became so very cold that the simpleton could scarcely bear to take a bath, and all the water in the room froze. So the simpleton wrapped himself up in the bath blankets, climbed upon the stove, and lay there the whole night. In the morning when they opened the door, there he lay sound and safe, singing cheerfully to himself.

Now when this strange tale was told to the king he became quite sad, not knowing what he should do to get rid of so undesirable a son-in-law, when suddenly an idea occurred to him.

"Tell the rascal to raise me an army, now at this instant!" he exclaimed to one of his courtiers. And to himself he added, "I think I shall foil him this time."

As on former occasions, the quick-eared comrade had overheard the king's command and repeated it to the simpleton.

"Alas, alas!" groaned the simpleton. "What shall I do? Now I am quite done for."

"Not at all," replied the comrade who had dragged the bundle of wood through the forest. "Have you quite forgotten me?"

In the meantime the courtier, who had run all the way from the palace, reached the ship panting and breathless, and he delivered the king's message.

"Good!" remarked the simpleton. "I will raise an army for the king," and he drew himself up. "But if, after that, the king refuses to accept me as his son-in-law, I will wage war against him and will carry the princess off by force."

During the night the simpleton and his comrade went together into a big field, not forgetting to take the bundle of wood with them, which the man spread out in all directions. In a moment a mighty army stood upon the spot, regiment upon regiment of foot and horse soldiers. The bugles sounded and the drums beat, the chargers neighed and their riders put their lances at rest, and the soldiers presented arms.

In the morning when the king awoke he was startled by these warlike sounds—the bugles and the drums, the clatter of the horses, and the shouts of the soldiers. Stepping to the window, he saw the lances gleam in the sunlight and the armor and weapons glitter. And the proud monarch said to himself, "I am powerless in comparison with this man." So he sent him royal robes and costly jewels, and he commanded him to come to the palace to be married to the princess. When the poor simpleton put on the royal robes, he looked so grand and stately that it was impossible to recognize him, so changed was he. And the princess fell in love with him as soon as ever she saw him.

Never before had so grand a wedding been seen, and there was so much food and wine that even the glutton and the thirsty comrade had enough to eat and drink.

Cinderella

here was once an honest widower who took for his second wife the proudest and most disagreeable lady in the whole country. She had two daughters exactly like herself. He himself had one little girl who resembled her mother, the best woman in all the world. Scarcely had the second marriage taken place before the stepmother became jealous of the good qualities of the little girl, who was so great a contrast to her own two daughters. She gave her all the hard work of the house—washing the floors and staircases, dusting the bedrooms, and cleaning the grates. While her sisters lived in carpeted chambers hung with mirrors in which they could see themselves from head to foot, this poor little girl was sent to sleep in an attic on an old straw mattress, with only one chair and not a looking glass in the room.

She suffered in silence, not daring to complain to her father, who was entirely ruled by his new wife. When her daily work was done she would sit down in the chimney corner among the cinders. Because of this, the two sisters gave her the nickname of Cinderella. But Cinderella, however shabbily clad, was still handsomer than they were, with all their fine clothes.

It happened that the king's son gave a series of balls, to which were invited all the rank and fashion of the city, and among them were the two elder sisters. They were very proud and happy, and they occupied all their time deciding what they should wear.

The important evening came, and Cinderella exercised all her skill in adorning the two young ladies. While she was combing out the elder's hair this ill-natured girl said sharply, "Cinderella, do you not wish you were going to the ball?"

"Ah, madam"—the sisters obliged Cinderella always to say madam—"you are only mocking me. It is not my fortune to have any such pleasure."

"You are right; people would only laugh to see a little cinder-wench at a ball."

After this, any other girl would have dressed her stepsister's hair all awry, but Cinderella was good and she made it perfectly even and smooth.

When at last the happy moment arrived, Cinderella followed them to the coach. Only after it had whirled them away did she sit down by the kitchen fire to cry.

Immediately her godmother, who was a fairy, appeared beside her. "What are you crying for, my little maid?"

"Oh, I wish—I wish—" Her sobs stopped her.

"You wish to go to the ball. Isn't it so?"

Cinderella nodded.

"Well then, be a good girl and you shall go. First run into the garden and fetch me the largest pumpkin you can find."

Cinderella did not understand what this had to do with her going to the ball, but being obedient, she went. Her godmother took the pumpkin, scooped out all its insides, and struck it with her wand. It then became a splendid gilt coach, lined with rose-colored satin.

"Now fetch me the mousetrap out of the pantry, my dear."

Cinderella brought it; it contained six of the fattest, furriest mice she'd ever seen.

The fairy lifted up the wire door, and as each mouse ran out she struck it and changed it into a beautiful horse.

"But what shall I do for your coachman, Cinderella?"

Cinderella said that she had seen a large black rat in the

rattrap, and she suggested he might do for lack of anything better.

"You are right. Go and look again for him."

He was found, and the fairy made him into a most respectable coachman with the finest whiskers imaginable. She then took six lizards from behind the carriage frame and changed them into six footmen, all in splendid livery, who immediately jumped up behind the carriage as if they had been footmen all their days.

"Well, Cinderella, now you can go to the ball."

"What, in these clothes?" said Cinderella sadly, looking down on her ragged frock.

Her godmother laughed and touched her with the wand. At once her wretched, threadbare jacket became stiff with gold and sparkling with jewels, and her woollen petticoat lengthened into a gown of sweeping satin. From underneath her gown peeped out her little feet, covered with silk stockings and the prettiest glass slippers in the world.

"Now, Cinderella, you may go. But remember, if you stay one instant after midnight your carriage will become a pumpkin, your coachman a rat, your horses mice, your footmen lizards, and you yourself will be the little cinder-wench again."

Without fear, Cinderella promised to obey her godmother's warning. And her heart was full of joy.

At the palace the prince had been told by someone—probably the fairy—to await the coming of an uninvited princess whom nobody knew. When Cinderella arrived, he was standing at the entrance, ready to receive her. He offered his hand and led her with the utmost courtesy through the assembled guests, who stood aside to let her pass, whispering to one another, "Oh, how beautiful she is!" Cinderella, who was so used to being despised, took it all as if it were something happening in a dream.

Her triumph was complete; even the old king said to the queen that never since Her Majesty's young days had he seen so charming a person. The prince led her out to dance, and she danced so gracefully that he admired her more and more. Indeed, at supper, his admiration quite took away his appetite. Cinderella herself sought out her sisters, placed herself beside them, and offered them all sorts of kind attentions. These, coming from a stranger (or so they supposed!) and so magnificent a lady, almost overwhelmed them with delight.

While Cinderella was talking with them, she heard the clock strike a quarter to twelve, and she bade a courteous *adieu* to the royal family. Escorted gallantly by the prince, she re-entered her carriage and arrived in safety at her own door. There she found her godmother, who smiled with approval. Cinderella begged her permission to go to a second ball the following night, to which the queen had invited her.

While she was talking, the two sisters were heard knocking at the gate, and the fairy godmother vanished, leaving Cinderella sitting in the chimney corner, rubbing her eyes and pretending to be very sleepy.

"Ah," cried the eldest sister spitefully, "it has been the most delightful ball, and there was present the most beautiful princess I ever saw, who was exceedingly polite to us both."

"Was she?" said Cinderella indifferently. "Who might she be?"

"Nobody knows, though everybody would give their eyes to know, especially the prince."

"Indeed!" replied Cinderella, a little more interested. "I should like to see her." Then she turned to the second sister and said, "Will you not let me go tomorrow, and lend me your yellow gown that you wear on Sundays?"

"What, lend my yellow gown to a cinder-wench? I am not so mad as that!" At which refusal Cinderella did not complain, for if her sister really had lent her the gown she would have been considerably embarrassed.

The next night came, and the two young ladies, richly dressed in different gowns, went to the ball. Cinderella, more splendidly attired and more beautiful than ever, followed them shortly after. "Now, remember, twelve o'clock," were her godmother's parting words, and Cinderella replied that she certainly would remember. But the prince's attentions to her were even greater than on

CINDERELLA

the first evening, and as she delighted in listening to his pleasant conversation, time slipped by unnoticed. While she was sitting beside him in a lovely alcove and looking at the moon from under a bower of orange blossom, she heard a clock strike the first stroke of twelve. She started up and fled away as lightly as a deer.

Amazed, the prince followed but could not catch her. Indeed, he missed his lovely princess altogether and only saw, running out of the palace doors, a little, dirty lass whom he had never beheld before, and of whom he would never have taken the least notice. Cinderella arrived at home breathless and weary, ragged and cold, without carriage or footmen or coachman. The only remnant of her past magnificence was one of her little glass slippers; the other she had dropped in the ballroom as she ran away.

When the two sisters returned they were full of this strange adventure—how the beautiful lady had appeared at the ball, how she was more beautiful than ever and enchanted everyone who looked at her, and how as the clock was striking twelve she had suddenly risen up and fled through the ballroom, disappearing (no one knew how or where!) and only leaving one of her glass slippers behind her in her flight.

The prince had been forlorn until he chanced to pick up the little glass slipper, which he carried away in his pocket. He was then seen to take it out continually and look at it affectionately, with the air of a man very much in love. In fact, from his behavior during the remainder of the evening, all the court and the royal family were sure that he was desperately in love with the wearer of the little glass slipper.

Cinderella listened in silence, turning her face to the kitchen fire. Perhaps it was that fire which made her look so rosy, but nobody at home even noticed. And so, the next morning she went to her weary work again, just as before.

A few days after, the whole city was attracted by the sight of a herald going around with a glass slipper in his hand. He announced, with a flourish of trumpets, that the prince ordered this to be fitted on the foot of every lady in the kingdom, and that he wished to marry the lady to whom it and its fellow slipper belonged. Princesses, duchesses, countesses, and simple gentlewomen all tried it on but, being a fairy slipper, it fitted nobody. Besides, nobody could produce its fellow slipper, which lay all the time safely in the pocket of Cinderella's old, woollen gown.

At last the herald came to the house of the two sisters and, though they well knew neither of them was the beautiful lady, they made every attempt to get their clumsy feet into the glass slipper, but in vain.

"Let me try it on," said Cinderella from the chimney corner.

"What, you?" cried the others, bursting into shouts of laughter. Cinderella only smiled and held out her hand.

Her sisters could not prevent her, since the command was that every maiden in the city should try on the slipper, in order that no chance to find the princess might be left untried. For the prince's heart was nearly broken, and his father and mother were afraid that he would actually die for love of the beautiful, unknown lady.

So the herald bade Cinderella sit down on a three-legged stool in the kitchen, and he himself put the slipper on her pretty little foot. It fitted exactly. She then drew from her pocket the other slipper, which she also put on, and stood up. With the touch of the magic shoes, all her dress was changed likewise. No longer was she the poor, despised cinder-wench, but the beautiful lady whom the prince loved.

Her sisters recognized her at once. Filled with astonishment and no little alarm, they threw themselves at her feet, begging her pardon for all their former unkindness. She embraced them, telling them she forgave them with all her heart and only hoped they would love her always. Then she departed with the herald to the king's palace, and she told her whole story to His Majesty and the royal family. They were not in the least surprised, for everybody believed in fairies, and everybody longed to have a fairy godmother.

As for the young prince, he found her more lovely and lovable than ever, and insisted upon marrying her immediately. Cinderella never went home again, but she sent for her two sisters and shortly after married them to two rich gentlemen of the court.

Jack and the Beanstalk

There was once upon a time a poor widow who had an only son named Jack and a cow named Milky White. All they had to live on was the milk the cow gave every morning, which they carried to the market and sold. But one morning Milky White gave no milk whatsoever.

"What shall we do, what shall we do?" said the widow, wringing her hands.

"Cheer up, Mother. I'll go and get work somewhere," said Jack.

"You've tried that before, and nobody would take you," said his mother. "We must sell Milky White and use the money to live on as best we can."

"All right, Mother," said Jack. "It's market day today, and I'll soon sell Milky White, and then we'll see what we can do."

So he took the cow's halter in his hand, and off he started. He hadn't gone far when he met a funny-looking old man who said to him, "Good morning, Jack."

"Good morning to you," said Jack, wondering how the man knew his name.

"Well, Jack, where are you off to?" said the man.

"I'm going to market to sell our cow."

"Oh, you look the proper sort of chap to sell cows," said the man. "I wonder if you know how many beans make five."

"Two in each hand and one in your mouth," said Jack, as sharp as a needle.

"Right you are," said the man. "And here they are, the very beans themselves. Then he pulled out of his pocket a number of strange-looking beans. "As you are so sharp," said he, "I don't mind doing a swap with you—your cow for these beans."

"Go along," said Jack.

"Ah! You don't know what these beans are," said the man. "If you plant them overnight, by morning they will grow right up to the sky."

"Really?" said Jack. "You don't say so!"

"Yes, that is so, and if it doesn't turn out to be true you can have your cow back."

"Right," said Jack, and he handed him over Milky White's halter and pocketed the beans.

So back home went Jack, much sooner than his mother expected.

"Back already, Jack?" said his mother. "I see you haven't got Milky White, so you've sold her. How much did you get for her?"

"You'll never guess, Mother," said Jack.

"Five pounds? Ten? Fifteen? No, it can't be twenty!"

"I told you you couldn't guess. What do you say to these beans? They're magical; plant them overnight and—"

"What?" said Jack's mother. "Have you been such a fool, such a dolt, such an idiot, as to give away my Milky White, the best milker in the parish—and prime beef to boot—for a set of paltry beans? Here they go out the window. And now off with you to your bed."

So Jack went upstairs to his little room in the attic, and sad and sorry he was, to be sure.

At last he dropped off to sleep.

When he woke up, what do you think he saw? Why, the beans his mother had thrown out the window had fallen into the garden and sprung up into a big beanstalk that went up and up and up till it reached the sky! So the old man spoke truth after all.

The beanstalk grew up quite close past Jack's window, so all he had to do was to open it and give a jump onto the beanstalk, which went up just like a big ladder. So Jack climbed and he climbed and he climbed and he climbed and he climbed and he climbed and he climbed till at last he reached the sky. When he got there he found a long, broad road going as straight as a dart. So he walked along and he walked along and he walked along till he came to a great big house, and on the doorstep there was a great big woman.

"Good morning, mum," said Jack, quite polite-like. "Could you be so kind as to give me some breakfast?" For, as you know, he hadn't had anything to eat the night before and was as hungry as a hunter.

"It's breakfast you want, is it?" said the great big woman. "It's breakfast you'll be if you don't move off from here. My man is an ogre and there's nothing he likes better than boys broiled on toast. You'd better be moving on or he'll soon be coming this way."

"Oh please, mum, do give me something to eat, mum. I've had nothing to eat since yesterday morning—really and truly, mum," said Jack. "I may as well be broiled as die of hunger."

Well, the ogre's wife was not half so bad after all. So she took Jack into the kitchen and gave him a chunk of bread and cheese and a jug of milk. But Jack hadn't half-finished these when *thump! thump! thump!* the whole house began to tremble with the noise of someone coming.

"Goodness gracious me! It's my husband," said the ogre's wife. "What on earth shall I do? Come along quickly and jump in here." And she bundled Jack into the oven just as the ogre came in.

He was a big one, to be sure. At his belt he had three calves strung up by the heels. As he unhooked them and threw them down on the table, he said: "Here, wife, broil me a couple of these for breakfast. Ah! What's this I smell?" And then he chanted:

> "Fee-fi-fo-fum,
> I smell the blood of an Englishman!
> Be he alive, or be he dead,
> I'll have his bones to grind my bread."

"Nonsense, dear," said his wife. "You're dreaming. Or perhaps you smell the scraps of that little boy you liked so much for yesterday's dinner. Here, you go and have a wash and tidy up, and by the time you come back, your breakfast'll be ready for you."

So off the ogre went, and Jack was just going to jump out of the oven and run away when the woman told him not to. "Wait till he's asleep," said she. "He always has a doze after breakfast."

Well, the ogre had his breakfast, and after that he went to a big chest and took out a couple of bags of gold. Then down he sat, and he counted his gold till at last his head began to nod. Soon he began to snore till the whole house shook again.

Then Jack crept out on tiptoe from his oven, and as he was passing the ogre he took one of the bags of gold from under his arm. Off he scampered till he came to the beanstalk, and then he threw down the bag of gold, which of course fell into his mother's garden. Then he climbed down and climbed down till at last he got home and told his mother all that happened. He showed her the gold and said, "Well, Mother, wasn't I right about the beans? They are really magical, you see."

So they lived on the bag of gold for some time, but at last they came to the end of it, and Jack made up his mind to try his luck once more up at the top of the beanstalk. So one fine morning he rose up early, got onto the beanstalk, and he climbed and he climbed and he climbed and he climbed and he climbed and he climbed till at last he came out onto the road again and up to the great big house he had been to before. There, sure enough, was the great big woman standing on the doorstep.

"Good morning, mum," said Jack, as bold as brass. "Could you be so good as to give me something to eat?"

"Go away, my boy," said the great big woman, "or else my man will eat you up for breakfast. But aren't you the youngster who came here once before? Do you know that on the very day you came here, my man missed one of his bags of gold?"

"That's strange, mum," said Jack. "I daresay I could tell you something about that, but I'm so hungry I can't speak till I've had something to eat."

Well, the great big woman was so curious that she took him in and gave him something to eat. But he had scarcely begun munching it when *thump! thump! thump!* they heard the giant's footsteps, and his wife hid Jack away in the oven.

All happened as it did before. In came the ogre again, and he said, "Fee-fi-fo-fum," and had his breakfast of three broiled oxen. Then he said, "Wife, bring me the hen that lays the golden eggs." So she brought it, and the ogre said, "Lay," and it laid an egg all of gold. Then the ogre began to nod his head and to snore till the house shook.

Then Jack crept out of the oven on tiptoe and caught hold of the golden hen, and he was off before you could say "Jack Robinson." But this time the hen gave a cackle that woke the ogre, and just as Jack got out of the house he heard the ogre calling, "Wife, wife, what have you done with my golden hen?"

But that was all Jack heard, for he rushed off to the beanstalk and climbed down as if it were a house on fire. And when he got home he showed his mother the wonderful hen and said, "Lay." And it laid a golden egg then and every time he said "Lay."

Well, Jack was not content, and it wasn't very long before he determined to have another try at his luck up at the top of the beanstalk. So one fine morning he rose up early and got onto the beanstalk, and he climbed and he climbed and he climbed and he climbed till he got to the top. But this time he knew better than to go straight to the ogre's house. And when he got near it, he waited behind a bush till he saw the ogre's wife come out with a pail to get some water, and then he crept into the house and got into the copper pot. He hadn't been there long when he heard *thump! thump! thump!* as before, and in came the ogre and his wife.

"Fee-fi-fo-fum, I smell the blood of an Englishman," cried the ogre. "I smell him, Wife, I smell him."

"Do you, my dearie?" said the ogre's wife. "Then if it's that little rogue who stole your gold and the hen that laid the golden eggs, he's sure to have gotten into the oven." And they both rushed to the oven. But Jack wasn't there, luckily, and the ogre's wife said, "There you are again with your 'fee-fi-fo-fum.' Why of

DOWN CLIMBS JACK

TROY·ALLYN·HOWELL

course it's the smell of the boy you caught last night that I've just broiled for your breakfast."

So the ogre sat down to the breakfast and ate it, but every now and then he would mutter, "Well, I could have sworn . . ." and he'd get up and search the larder and the cupboards, and many other places. Luckily he didn't think of the copper pot.

After breakfast was over, the ogre called out, "Wife, bring me my golden harp!" So she brought it and put it on the table before him. Then he said, "Sing!" and the golden harp sang most beautifully. And it went on singing till the ogre fell asleep and began to snore like thunder.

Then Jack lifted up the copper lid very quietly, got down like a mouse, and crept on hands and knees till he came to the table. Then up he crawled, caught hold of the golden harp, and dashed with it toward the door. But the harp called out quite loudly, "Master! Master!" and the ogre woke up just in time to see Jack running off with his harp.

Jack ran as fast as he could, but the ogre came rushing after him. When Jack got to the beanstalk, the ogre was not more than twenty yards away. Suddenly the ogre saw Jack disappear, and when he came to the end of the road he saw Jack underneath, climbing down for dear life. Well, the ogre didn't trust such a ladder, so he stood and waited. But just then the harp cried out, "Master! Master!" and the ogre swung himself down onto the beanstalk, which shook with his weight.

Down climbed Jack, and after him climbed the ogre. By this time Jack had climbed down and climbed down till he was very nearly home. So he called out, "Mother! Mother! Bring me an ax!" And his mother came rushing out with the ax in her hand.

Jack jumped down, got hold of the ax, and gave a chop at the beanstalk. When Jack gave it another chop, the beanstalk was cut in two and began to topple over. Then the ogre fell down and broke his crown, and the beanstalk came toppling after.

Then Jack showed his mother his golden harp, and by playing that and selling the golden eggs, Jack and his mother became very rich, and he married a great princess, and they lived happy ever after.

The Selfish Giant

very afternoon as they were coming from school, the children used to go and play in the giant's garden.

It was a large, lovely garden with soft, green grass. Here and there over the grass stood beautiful flowers like stars, and there were twelve peach trees that in the springtime broke out into delicate blossoms of pink and pearl, and in the autumn they bore rich fruit. The birds sat on the trees and sang so sweetly that the children used to stop their games in order to listen to them. "How happy we are here!" they cried to one another.

One day the giant came back. He had been to visit his friend the Cornish ogre, and he had stayed with him for seven years. After the seven years were over, he had said all that he had to say, for his conversation was limited, and he determined to return to his own castle. When he arrived he saw the children playing in the garden.

"What are you doing here?" he cried in a very gruff voice, and the children ran away.

"My own garden is my own garden," said the giant. "Anyone can understand that, and I will allow nobody to play in it but myself." So he built a high wall all round it, and put up a notice board:

TRESPASSERS
WILL BE
PROSECUTED

He was a very selfish giant.

The poor children now had nowhere to play. They tried to play on the road, but the road was very dusty and full of hard stones, and they did not like it. They used to wander outside the high walls when their lessons were over, and they would talk about the beautiful garden inside. "How happy we were there!" they said to one another.

Then the Spring came, and all over the country there were little blossoms and little birds. Only in the garden of the selfish giant was it still winter. The birds did not care to sing in it as there were no children, and the trees forgot to blossom. Once a beautiful flower put its head out from the grass, but when it saw the notice board it was so sorry for the children that it slipped back into the ground again and went off to sleep. The only people who were pleased were the Snow and the Frost. "Spring has forgotten this garden," they cried, "so we will live here all year round." The Snow covered up the grass with her great white cloak, and the Frost painted all the trees silver. Then they invited the North Wind to stay with them, and he came. He was wrapped in furs, and he roared all day about the garden, blowing the chimney pots down in the giant's fireplace.

"This is a delightful spot," he said. "We must ask the Hail to visit." So the Hail came. Every day for three hours he rattled on the roof of the castle till he broke most of the slates, and then he ran around and around the garden as fast as he could go. He was dressed in gray and his breath was like ice.

"I cannot understand why the Spring is so late in coming," said the selfish giant, as he sat at the window and looked out at his cold white garden. "I hope there will be a change in the weather."

But the Spring never came, nor the Summer. The Autumn gave golden fruit to every garden, but to the giant's garden she gave none. "He is too selfish," she said. So it was always winter there, and the North Wind and the Hail, and the Frost, and the Snow danced about through the trees.

One morning the giant was lying awake in bed when he heard some lovely music. It sounded so sweet to his ears that he thought it must be the king's musicians passing by. It was really only a little linnet singing outside his window, but it was so long since he had heard a bird sing in his garden that it seemed to him to be the most beautiful music in the world. Then the Hail stopped dancing over his head, and the North Wind ceased roaring, and a delicious perfume came to him through the open casement. "I believe the Spring has come at last," said the giant; and he jumped out of bed and looked out.

What did he see?

He saw a most wonderful sight. Through a little hole in the wall the children had crept in, and they were sitting in the branches of the trees. In every tree that he could see, there was a little child. And the trees were so glad to have the children back again that they had covered themselves with blossoms and were waving their arms gently above the children's heads. The birds were flying about and twittering with delight, and the flowers were looking up through the green grass and laughing. It was a lovely scene, only in one corner it was still winter. It was the farthest corner of the garden, and in it was standing a little boy. He was so small that he could not reach up to the branches of the tree, and he was wandering all round it, crying bitterly. The poor tree was still covered with frost and snow, and the North Wind was blowing and roaring above it. "Climb up, little boy," said the tree, and it bent its branches down as low as it could; but the boy was too tiny.

The giant's heart melted as he looked out. "How selfish I have been!" he said. "Now I know why the Spring would not come here. I will put that poor little boy on the top of the tree, and then I will knock down the wall, and my garden shall be the children's playground forever and ever." He was really very sorry for what he had done.

So he crept downstairs, opened the front door quite softly, and

TRESPASSERS
WILL BE
PROSECUTED

TROY·ALLYN·HOWELL

went out into the garden. But when the children saw him they were so frightened that they all ran away, and the garden became winter again. Only the little boy did not run, for his eyes were so full of tears that he did not see the giant coming. The giant stole up behind him, took him gently in his hand, and put him up into the tree. The tree broke at once into blossom, and the birds came and sang on it, and the little boy stretched out his two arms, flung them round the giant's neck, and kissed him. And the other children, when they saw that the giant was not wicked any longer, came running back, and with them came the Spring. "It is your garden now, little children," said the giant, and he took a great ax and knocked down the wall. And when the people were going to market at twelve o'clock, they found the giant playing with the children in the most beautiful garden they had ever seen.

All day long they played, and in the evening they came to the giant to bid him good-bye.

"But where is your little companion," he said, "the boy I put into the tree?" The giant loved him the best because the child had kissed him.

"We don't know," answered the children. "He has gone away."

"You must tell him to be sure and come tomorrow," said the giant. But the children said that they did not know where he lived and had never seen him before; and the giant felt very sad.

Every afternoon when school was over, the children came and played with the giant. But the little boy whom the giant loved was never seen. The giant was very kind to all the children, yet he longed for his first little friend and often spoke of him. "How I would like to see him!" he used to say.

Years went over, and the giant grew very old and feeble. He could not play about anymore, so he sat in a huge armchair, watching the children at their games and admiring his garden. "I have many beautiful flowers," he said, "but the children are the most beautiful flowers of all."

One winter morning he looked out of his window as he was dressing. He did not hate the Winter now, for he knew that it was merely the Spring asleep, and that the flowers were resting.

Suddenly he rubbed his eyes in wonder, and he looked and

looked. It certainly was a marvelous sight. In the farthest corner of the garden was a tree quite covered with lovely white blossoms. Its branches were golden, and silver fruit hung down from them, and underneath it stood the little boy he had loved.

Downstairs ran the giant in great joy, and out into the garden. He hastened across the grass and came near to the child. But when he came quite close his face grew red with anger, and he said, "Who hath dared to wound thee?" For on the palms of the child's hands were the prints of two nails, and the prints of two nails were on the little feet.

"Who hath dared to wound thee?" cried the giant. "Tell me, that I may take my big sword and slay him."

"Nay," answered the child, "but these are the wounds of Love."

"Who art thou?" said the giant, and a strange awe fell on him, and he knelt before the little child.

And the child smiled on the giant, and said to him, "You let me play once in your garden. So today you shall come with me to my garden, which is paradise."

And when the children ran to play that afternoon, they found the giant lying dead under the tree, all covered with white blossoms.

East of the Sun and West of the Moon

nce upon a time there was a poor man who had many children and little to give them in the way of either food or clothing. They were all pretty, but the prettiest of all was the youngest daughter.

One day they were all sitting together by the fireside, each of them busy with something, when suddenly someone rapped three times against the windowpane. The man went out to see what could be the matter, and when he went out, there stood a great big white bear.

"Good evening to you," said the white bear.

"Good evening," said the man.

"Will you give me your youngest daughter?" said the white bear. "If you will, you shall be as rich as you are now poor."

Truly the man would have had no objection to be rich, but he thought to himself, "I must first ask my daughter about this." So he went in and told the children that there was a great white bear outside who had faithfully promised to make them all rich if he might but have the youngest daughter.

She said no and would not hear of it; so the man went out again and settled with the white bear that he should come again next Thursday evening to get her answer. Then the man tried to persuade her. He talked so much to her about the wealth that they would have, and what a good thing it would be for herself, that at last she made up her mind to go. She washed and mended all her rags and made herself as smart as she could.

The next Thursday evening the white bear came to fetch her. She seated herself on his back with her bundle, and thus they departed.

"Keep tight hold of my fur, and then there is no danger," said he. Then they were off.

And they rode far, far away, until they came to a great mountain. Then the white bear knocked on it and a door opened, and they went into a castle where there were many brilliantly lit rooms that shone with gold and silver. The white bear gave the girl a silver bell and told her that when she needed anything she had but to ring this bell; what she wanted would then appear. So after she had eaten and night was drawing near, she grew sleepy after her long journey and thought she would like to go to bed. She rang the bell, and scarcely had she touched it before she found herself in a chamber where a bed stood ready-made for her. But when she had lain down and put out the light, a man came and lay down beside her—it was the white bear, who cast off the form of a beast during the night. He came each night, but she never saw him, for he always came after she had put out her light, and he went away before daylight appeared.

So all went well and happily for a time, but then she began to be very sad and sorrowful, for all day long she had to go about alone; and she did so wish to go home to her father and mother and brothers and sisters. Then the white bear asked what it was that she wanted. She told him that it was so dull there in the mountain, and that she had to go about all alone, and that in her parents' house were all her brothers and sisters, and that it was because she could not go to them that she was so sorrowful.

"There might be a cure for that," said the white bear, "if you would but promise me never to talk with your mother alone, but only when the others are there too. For she will take hold of your hand and will want to lead you into a room to talk with you alone. And that you must by no means do, or you will bring great misery on both of us."

So one Sunday the white bear came and said that they could now set out to see her father and mother for the day, and they journeyed thither, she sitting on his back. They went a long, long way, and it took a long, long time, but at last they came to a large white farmhouse. Her brothers and sisters were running about outside it, playing, and it was so pretty that it was a pleasure to look at.

"Your parents dwell here now," said the white bear. "But do not forget what I said to you, or you will do much harm to yourself and me."

"No indeed," said she. "I shall never forget." And as soon as she was at home, the white bear turned around and went back again.

When she went in to her parents, there were such rejoicings that it seemed as if they would never come to an end. Now they had everything that they wanted, and everything was as good as it could be. They all asked her how she was getting along where she was. All was well with her too, she said; she had everything that she could want.

But in the afternoon, after they had dined at midday, all happened just as the white bear had said. Her mother wanted to talk with her alone in her own chamber. But the girl remembered what the white bear had said, and she would on no account go. "What we have to say can be said at any time," the girl answered. But somehow or other her mother at last persuaded her, and she was forced to tell the whole story. So she told how every night a man came and lay down beside her when the lights were all put out, and how she never saw him because he always went away before it grew light in the morning, and how she continually went about in sadness, thinking how happy she would be if she could but see him, and how all day long she had to go about alone, and it was so dull and solitary.

"Oh!" cried the mother in horror. "You are very likely sleeping with a troll! But I will teach you a way to see him. You shall have a bit of one of my candles, which you can take away with you hidden in your breast. Look at him with that when he is asleep, but take care not to let any wax drop upon him."

So she took her mother's candle and hid it in her breast, and when evening drew near the white bear came to fetch her away. When they had gone some distance on their way, the white bear asked her if everything had not happened just as he had foretold, and she could not but own that it had.

"Then if you have done what your mother wished," said he, "you will bring great misery on both of us."

"No," said she. "I have not done anything at all." So when she had reached home and had gone to bed it was just the same as it had been before, and a man came and lay down beside her. But late at night when she could hear that he was sleeping, she got up and lit her candle, let her light shine on him, and saw that he was the handsomest prince that eyes had ever beheld. She loved him so much that it seemed to her she must die if she did not kiss him that very moment. So she did kiss him, but while she was doing it she let three drops of hot wax fall upon his shirt, and he awoke.

"What have you done now?" said he. "You have brought misery on both of us. If you had but held out for one year I would have been free. I have a stepmother who has bewitched me so that I am a white bear by day and a man by night; but now all is at an end between you and me, and I must leave you and go to her. She lives in a castle which lies east of the sun and west of the moon. There too lives a princess with a nose that is as long as three eels, and she now is the one whom I must marry."

The girl wept and lamented but all in vain, for go he must. Then she asked him if she could go with him. But no, that could not be. "Can you tell me the way then, and I will seek you. That I may surely be allowed to do!"

"Yes, you may do that," said he, "but there is no way thither. It lies east of the sun and west of the moon, and never would you find your way there."

When she awoke in the morning both the prince and the castle were gone, and she was lying on a small, green patch in the midst of a dark, thick wood. By her side lay the selfsame bundle of rags which she had brought with her from her own home. So when she had rubbed the sleep out of her eyes and wept till she was weary, she set out on her way. She walked for many and many a long day, until at last she came to a great mountain. Outside it, an aged woman was sitting, playing with a golden apple. The girl asked her if she knew the way to the prince who lived with his stepmother in the castle that lay east of the sun and west of the moon, and who was to marry a princess with a nose that was as long as three eels.

"How do you happen to know about him?" enquired the old woman. "Maybe you are the one who ought to have married him."

"Yes, indeed, I am," she said.

"So it is you, then?" said the old woman. "I know nothing about him; but you shall have the loan of my horse, and then you can ride on it to an old woman who is a neighbor of mine. Perhaps she can tell you about him. When you have got what you need, you must just strike the horse beneath the left ear and bid it go home again. Here, you may take the golden apple with you."

So the girl seated herself on the horse and rode for a long, long way. At last she came to the mountain, where an aged woman was sitting outside with a gold carding comb. The girl asked her if she knew the way to the castle that lay east of the sun and west of the moon, but the woman said she did not.

"But you shall have the loan of my horse to an old woman who lives the nearest to me; perhaps she may know where the castle is." Then the old woman gave the girl her gold carding comb, saying it might perhaps be of use to her.

So the girl seated herself on the horse and rode a wearisome, long way onward again. After a very long time she came to a great mountain, where an aged woman was sitting, spinning at a golden spinning wheel. Of this woman, too, she enquired about the way to the prince, and where to find the castle that lay east of the sun and west of the moon. But this old crone knew the way no better than the others. It was east of the sun and west of the moon, she knew that, "and you will be a long time in getting to it, if ever you get to it at all," she said. "But you may have the loan of my horse, and I think you had better ride to the East Wind, and ask him. Perhaps he may know where the castle is and will blow you thither." And then she gave the girl the golden

THUS SHE RODE FAR, FAR, AWAY

TROY · ALLYN · HOWELL

spinning wheel, saying that she might find use for it.

The girl had to ride for a great many days, and for a long and wearisome time, before she got there. When at last she did arrive, she asked the East Wind if he could tell her the way to the prince who dwelt east of the sun and west of the moon.

"Well," said the East Wind, "I have heard tell of the prince and of his castle, but I do not know the way to it, for I have never blown so far. But if you like, I will go with you to my brother the West Wind. He may know the way, for he is much stronger than I am."

So the girl seated herself on his back, and they did go so swiftly! When they got there, the East Wind went in and said that the girl whom he had brought was the one who ought to have married the prince up at the castle that lay east of the sun and west of the moon, and that now she was traveling about to find him again and would like to hear if the West Wind knew the whereabouts of the castle.

"No," said the West Wind. "So far as that have I never blown. But if you like, I will go with you to the South Wind, for he is much stronger than either of us, and he has roamed far and wide, and perhaps he can tell you what you want to know."

So they journeyed to the South Wind, and when they got there, the West Wind asked him if he could tell her the way to the castle that lay east of the sun and west of the moon.

"Well," said he, "I have wandered about a great deal in my time, and in all kinds of places, but I have never blown so far as that. If you like, however, I will go with you to my brother the North Wind. He is the oldest and strongest of all of us, and if he does not know where it is, no one in the whole world will be able to tell you."

So she seated herself on his back, and off he went from his house in great haste, and they were not long on the way. When they came near the North Wind's dwelling, he was so wild and frantic that they felt cold gusts a long while before they got there.

"What do you want?" he roared out from afar, and they froze as they heard him.

Said the South Wind, "It is I, and this is she who should have married the prince who lives in the castle that lies east of the sun and west of the moon. And now she wishes to ask you if you have ever been there and can tell her the way, for she would gladly find him again."

"Yes," said the North Wind, "I know where it is. I once blew an aspen leaf there, but I was so tired that for many days afterward I was not able to blow at all. However, if you really are anxious to go there and are not afraid to go with me, I will take you on my back and try to blow you there."

"Get there I must," said the girl, "and if there is any way of going I will. I have no fear, no matter how fast you go."

"Very well, then," said the North Wind, "but you must sleep here tonight, for if we are ever to get there we must have the day before us."

The North Wind woke her early next morning. Then he puffed himself up and made himself so big and so strong that it was frightful to see him, and away they went, high up through the air, as if they would not stop until they had reached the very end of the world. Thus they tore on and on, and a long time went by, and then yet more time passed and still they were above the sea. The North Wind grew tired, and more tired, and at last so utterly weary that he was scarcely able to blow any longer. Then he sank and sank, lower and lower, until at last he went so low that the crests of the waves dashed against the heels of the poor girl he was carrying.

"Art thou afraid?" said the North Wind.

"I have no fear," said she, and it was true. But they were not very, very far from land, and there was just enough strength left in the North Wind to enable him to throw her onto the shore, immediately under the windows of a castle that lay east of the sun and west of the moon.

On the next morning she sat down beneath the walls of the castle to play with the golden apple, and the first person she saw was the maiden with the long nose who was to marry the prince.

"How much do you want for that golden apple of yours, girl?" said she, opening the window.

"It can't be bought for either gold or money," answered the girl.

"If it cannot be bought for either gold or money, what will buy it?" said the princess.

"Well, if I may go to the prince who is here, and be with him tonight, you shall have it," said the girl who had come with the North Wind.

"You may do that," said the princess, for she had made up her mind what she would do. So the princess got the golden apple, but when the girl went up to the prince's apartment that night he was asleep, for the princess had so planned it. The poor girl called to him and shook him throughout the night, and all the while she wept, but she could not wake him.

As soon as day dawned the next morning, in came the princess with the long nose, and she drove the girl out again.

So the girl sat down once more beneath the windows of the castle, and she began to card with her golding carding comb; and then all happened as it had happened before. The princess asked her what she wanted for it, and she replied that it was not for sale, for either gold or money, but that if she could have leave to go to the prince and be with him during the night, the princess should have it. But when she went up to the prince's room he was again asleep, and even though she called him, shook him, or wept as she would, he still slept on and she could not put any life in him.

When daylight came in the morning, the princess with the long nose came too and once more drove her away. Again the girl seated herself under the castle windows, but this time she spun with her golden spinning wheel, and the princess with the long nose wanted to have that spinning wheel too. So she opened the window and asked what the girl would take for it. The girl said what she had said on each of the former occasions—that it was not for sale for either gold or money, but if she could have leave to go to the prince and be with him during the night, she should have it.

"Yes," said the princess. "I will gladly consent to that."

But in that very castle there were some villagers who had been taken there as prisoners, and they had been sitting in the chamber next to that of the prince. Each night they had heard a woman in there who had wept and called on the prince two nights running, and they told him of this. So that evening, when the princess came once more with his nightly drink, he pretended to drink, but threw it away behind him, for he suspected that it was a sleeping drink. So when the girl went into the prince's room this time, he was awake, and she had to tell him how she had come there.

"You have come just in time," said the prince, "for I should have been married tomorrow. But I will not have the long-nosed princess, and you alone can save me. I will say that I want to see what my bride can do, and I'll bid her wash the shirt that has the three drops of wax on it. This she will consent to do, and then I will say that no one shall ever be my bride but the woman who can wash the wax off the shirt. I know that only you can do this."

There was great joy and gladness between them all that night, but the next day, when the wedding was to take place, the prince said, "I must see what my bride can do."

"That you may do," said the stepmother.

"I have a fine shirt which I want to wear as my wedding shirt, but upon it are three drops of wax that I want to have washed off, and I have vowed to marry no one but the woman who is able to do it. If she cannot do this, she is not worth having."

"Well, that is a very small matter," thought the stepmother, and she told the princess, who agreed to do it. The princess with the long nose began to wash as well as she could, but the more she washed and rubbed, the larger the spots grew.

"Ah! you can't wash at all," said her mother, an old troll-hag. "Give it to me." But she too had not had the shirt very long in her hands before it looked worse still, and the more she washed it and rubbed it, the larger and blacker grew the spots.

Soon the other trolls came to help wash, but the more they tried, the blacker and uglier grew the shirt, until at length it was as black as if it had been up the chimney.

"Oh," cried the prince when he saw it, "not one of you is good for anything at all! There is a beggar girl sitting outside the window, and I'll be bound that she can wash better than any of you! Come in, you girl there!" he cried.

"Oh! I don't know," said she, "but I will try." And no sooner had she taken the shirt and dipped it in the water than it was white as driven snow, and even whiter than that.

"I will marry you," said the prince.

Then the old troll-hag flew into such a rage that she burst, and the princess with the long nose and all the little trolls must have burst too, for they have never been heard of since. The prince and his bride set free all the villagers who were imprisoned there. Then they took away with them all the gold and silver that they could carry, and moved far away from the castle that lay east of the sun and west of the moon.